CW00661417

Guilt Edged

P. R. McKnight

Copyright © 2022 P. R. McKnight

All rights reserved.

ISBN: 9798435586916

Acknowledgements

My thanks to my long suffering wife, who has found herself reading several rewrites of the story willingly and without complaint. Mostly.

Thanks to Tracy, who helped with dream interpretation "mumbo jumbo." She is tall and blond, but not particularly hell-bent on vengeance, although that may change after she reads the book.

Thanks to Gabby Heycock, of the Oxfordshire Fire Brigade, for advice on what happens after somebody sets fire to your property.

Thanks to Ross Speirs, recently retired bicycle wheel builder of this parish, who was in no way responsible for the cycling puns, but did offer some very useful constructive criticism. I anticipated the question, "Why is this story set in 2018, not 'now'?" The answer is because I wanted it to be pre pandemic. I figured it was going to be hard enough to follow without everybody talking through masks.

Thanks to Anthony Forbes-Watson for putting me in touch with Bella Pagan at Pan Publishing, and thanks to her and Georgia for their constructive criticism and advice.

Author's photograph by Dee Robinson.

Contents

Prologue

What do you say to a vengeance demon whose declared purpose is to ruin your life, but has very generously just bought you a double espresso and a Chelsea bun? I don't know if they're all going to be like the one I met. He was very critical of my table manners and offended by my swearing, but my advice would be, if you should ever meet one, choose your words carefully. I didn't fancy being on the receiving end of a display of his power, which I'd already discovered was considerable. It didn't seem likely that talking with my mouth full would be enough to have him unleash this on me, but you never know.

But please don't think this was merely a chance encounter in a café; a man and a vengeance demon walk into a coffee bar. It's been no joke, believe me…...

A Room With No View

I have to get out of this room. I don't know why I do, but I just know that I have to get out of the place as fast as I possibly can. The only way I can see is through that single window in the corner. It's an old sash window and I really hope that years of repeated careless decorating haven't left it painted shut. That always seems to happen to those old sash windows.

What am I thinking? Of course I can get out there; that's the way I got into the bloody room in the first place. I have to keep my head. This desperate urge to escape is pushing me to irrational panic. Mustn't panic. It's not helping. I fumble with the tarnished metal catch on the window, which, eventually, reluctantly, opens, and then I painfully graze my fingers as I strain to push the lower frame up in its channels. Shit! That'll hurt later more than it does now.

In spite of my extreme anxiety, there is nothing that can be described as even the slightest bit intimidating about this room. I can't say that I go a bundle on the style and quality of its fixtures and fittings: the faded orange and yellow flowery curtains which clash with the rather busy paisley patterned red carpet. The walls have that most basic of coverings, woodchip painted magnolia or buttermilk; I'm not sure which colour it is. It's cheap and cheerless and hasn't really covered up the damp patches very well. The carpet has seen much better days and it's become threadbare and worn, but there's still enough of it to cover the uneven slopes of a creaky wooden floor. A light oak dresser is the only item of furniture. So, nothing scary here. It's the slightly open door into the next room that concerns me.

Standing on the oak dresser, alongside a couple of porcelain figurines of a little boy and girl having a picnic and a very unrealistic blue tit hanging upside down from a branch, it's all a bit twee for my liking, there is a small blue-white ceramic pot with a healthy looking miniature rose, adorned with tight yellow buds. I've brushed my fingers across the soil in the pot and it felt moist enough to confirm that somebody cares for the plant. Somebody comes here regularly. And there's not a speck of dust. Those ghastly ornaments are usually dust magnets, I think. Not sure why I should be concerned about that, except that I have a bit of a thing about dust; I love the sunshine, but it really shows up the dust, and I find it hard.....oh come on! This isn't really helping me one bit, wasting time appraising somebody else's housekeeping standards. It's that adjoining room that still bothers me, even though I can't hear a sound coming from it, or, for that matter, anywhere else.

The door to the other room isn't open wide enough for me to see in, and I'm not sure I want to anyway, but I feel a sense of menace. Menace? Maybe, or is it simply that I don't want to be discovered here? That feeling of guilt brought on by being somewhere I'm not supposed to be? Is there an intruder, or am I the intruder?

Like I said, I have to get out.

The opened window just about allows me enough space to push my head and shoulders through, to look outside and find an escape route. Logically, I should retrace my steps; that would make sense, but that suddenly appears to be easier said than done. I find it hard to believe that this is the way I came in. I couldn't have climbed through a window this far up. It's at least twenty feet to the ground, but a few feet to my right there is a wall at right angles to the building, dividing it from the next property. If I could lower myself over the sill I should be able to reach the top of the wall with one foot; shouldn't be too difficult. As a rule, I'm not particularly scared of climbing, but my target is a narrow strip of crumbling brickwork, old and mossy and made slippery by recent rain. It doesn't look safe, but then jumping twenty feet is out of the question too.

This doesn't make any sense. It puzzles me how I could possibly have got in this way. I'm struggling to balance the fear of falling against the fear of whatever may be in that adjoining room. It might make more sense to go back and find out what it is, what's in the room. My mouth is so dry. I could do with a drink of water.

I reach out to feel for the glass on my bedside table. Hot and thirsty; well that's how I usually feel if I wake up in the early hours of the morning, disturbed by the critical moment in a bad dream. A sort of fight or flight moment. Typical! I would have to wake in the middle of a cliffhanger, although to be fair, that's probably rather a grandiose way of describing trying to balance on a garden wall.

I turn over to check the time on the alarm clock. It's just gone four and suddenly I'm wide awake and aware of my surroundings. I'm lying in bed next to my wife, Trish. At this time of the night she's in a deep sleep and doesn't react to me moving.

So; the window dream again. I should be used to it,

3

but that's not how dreams work and it's disturbingly real when I'm there. Unsettled, I decide to get up and go downstairs for the rest of the night. It's a habit I've got into. I'm not sure if it's a good habit, but if I have to live with insomnia I might as well do something I enjoy with all this spare time.

My hand reaches out in the dark and locates my dressing gown with the certain aim of years of practice. Moving as quietly as I can, missing out the noisy third from top stair tread, I reach the ground floor and switch on a small table lamp; not enough light to flood the house, but sufficient for me to be able to select something from my vinyl record collection. Tonight I decide it will be Brand X, a bit of jazz-rock fusion to fascinate me, or maybe to clutter up my mind with something other than the recent dream so I can enjoy a couple more hours' sleep. I switch on my hi-fi and plug my trusty Sony headphones into the output jack. There's no need to wake the whole house, or the one next door. As I stretch out on the sofa I speculate whether my hearing will outlive my need to listen to music in the middle of the night. I close my eyes as the first slightly challenging bars of Nightmare Patrol filter into my senses. Why did I have to pick that one?

My mind starts to lose its focus and sleep comes creeping again. I can't pinpoint the moment when I drift off. Well you can't, can you? I've discovered that I'm able to do so in hindsight, by remembering which tracks on my records I did and didn't hear. That's not completely useless information; at least I know then I can't come out with the old "I didn't sleep a wink last night" chestnut. Okay, almost useless information. But just as I lose consciousness, I glimpse a first floor window, and the movement of a faded orange and yellow curtain being pulled back.

Living The Dream 1

More often than not these days, I spend much of the night on the sofa, and I know that sounds like the clichéd sleeping arrangements of a couple who have been together too long. But that's not the case with Trisha and me at all. It's just my practical way of dealing with my frequent insomnia. When I wake in what are commonly known as ungodly hours, I get restless and I start fidgeting. Not wanting to interrupt Trisha's much valued sleep, that's why I sneak out of the bedroom and down the stairs to my dark brown leather, three seater refuge.

Our day together starts around eight. It's time for our coffee ritual. Ignoring whatever the health implications are for starting the day with two large mugs, each that is, of strong coffee, that's what we always do. I whizz up the beans in the grinder and fill the cafetière, place the mugs, milk and sugar on a round aluminium tray and head for the dining room table. We can sit there with a good view of the garden, watching the birds' activities on the feeders, or log in to the BBC News page on our ever open laptop and discuss whatever they decide to tell us is new in the world. Yes, it's a bit of a ritual, but it's our ritual.

This morning, as the coffee grinder goes silent, I hear the door into the dining room open and Trisha walks in. I turn to greet her.

"Hello, lover."
"Morning."

She stretches and yawns and then shakes her head to try to synchronise herself with the new day which, even at eight o'clock, has started too early for her. Her hair, which she would describe as all over the place and in need of sorting out and I would describe as her wild Gypsy look, sways across her shoulders. She walks over to me, I put my arms around her waist and we kiss. I can tell she thinks I need a shave.

"Sleep well?" she asks, pulling back slightly, prepared for another one of my 'you'll never guess what I dreamed about last night' yarns. For now I'll spare her and keep it simple.

"Not too bad. How about you?"

"Pretty good. I think I heard you going downstairs at about four."

So much for thinking about the noisy stair tread……

"But I soon got back to sleep; not a problem."

I'm a happy man. I haven't always been. Who is? But my route to my present state of wedded bliss has been far from easy. There have been relationship disasters along the way and it pains me to say that I have been as guilty as anyone of causing those disasters. But this coffee won't drink itself…..

It's coffee, in a way, that brought us together in the first place, although our initial encounter had more to do with paint stripper than coffee. Not as a beverage, obviously, but I'd had to visit the local police station to provide details after somebody had poured chemicals all over my car's bodywork. Nothing ever came of that "investigation": (Did I have any enemies? A vindictive ex perhaps? Yes, but driving two hundred miles to deface my car wasn't her style.) Trisha had nothing to do with it either. We just happened to go for the same space in the car park and, being a perfect gent when I saw somebody I really fancied, I conceded the space and got a lovely smile for my generosity.

It was a complete coincidence that we both finished up working in a busy café in the small town where we live. ("Oh! It's you!") I was cooking the breakfasts and lunches and Trisha, answering an advert, signed up for a few front of house shifts. Her perfectionist's approach to making cappuccinos and flat whites transferred well to assisting me in my valiant attempts to produce attractive meals during busy lunchtimes. I'm quite competent as a cook, nobody's come back to complain, but I'm honest enough to admit that I'll never be in the Heston Blumenthal or Gordon Ramsey league, although swearing under pressure is something I'm very good at. Trisha turned out to be every bit as good as me at cooking, and swearing, and it wasn't long before our work-life balance tipped over into the dual tasks of cooking by day and, during our spare time, looking for somewhere we could live together. We bared all in our conversations; the failed relationships and consequent movement round the country. Over the years we'd both developed very strong ideas about what we did and didn't want in our lives. The upshot of this was that we decided that what we wanted now was each other, figuring that we could make less of a hash of our future than our past if the future was together; a bit like our cooking really. So, drawing up a list of key ingredients, we became an item, which I've always thought sounds like something you would find in the minutes of a parish council meeting, but it was a lot more romantic than that.

Our minutes became hours, and so on.

Funny, isn't it? Not laugh out loud funny; more funny peculiar, I mean. Suddenly it seems, I'm in a new world, happy and stable with a loving wife, a comfortable home, gainfully self-employed and hardly a trace of the life I left behind to be seen anywhere. Is it selfish to be happy and just shut the door on the past? Are the people in my past, some of whom I've hurt badly, still hurting? Do they even think about me, for good or bad? I'm not sure I can really afford to entertain these thoughts. I've grown up and moved on. Life's good for me now. Good for me…

Chris and Trisha; I joked that we sounded like the start of a sneezing fit, but my poor jokes didn't prevent Trisha from agreeing to marry me, and she gives every indication that she is as happy as I am. Well, we talk about "us" a lot, so that's how I know.

But something else we talk about, less frequently, is the incident that led to our first encounter in the car park near the police station. We never did find out who treated my car to a Nitromors bath, nor who, almost as soon as it was returned from the body shop, saw fit to slash all four tyres. My bank account took quite a hit that year, and I cursed and swore as profusely as my skill set would allow, but, as with the paint stripper incident, no culprit was found. As before, the police asked me about possible vendettas and, as before, I couldn't help with their inquiries. There wasn't much of a network of CCTV back in the Noughties and, as it wasn't exactly the crime of the century, the local constabulary promised to keep their eyes open and keep a file open. In the decade or so that has passed, the file has probably worked its way to the back of the cabinet to grow old and dusty. Curiously, that was that as regards attacks on my car; perhaps they were simply random incidents. Maybe I'd unwittingly been the catalyst for an outbreak of road rage; who knows?

Coffee's getting cold. It's Sunday, and we're not working.

"Any plans for today?" Trisha asks.

"Nothing specific. Fancy breakfast in Marlow? Walk by the river, see how the local ducks are getting on; that sort of thing?"

You see? Like I said before; wedded bliss. The scenario may appear to lack excitement, but what do you want out of life? Car chases? Living on your wits to escape the threats from your local drugs cartel? Our cosy little cottage in this small Oxfordshire market town isn't built on a hell mouth. Sorry if that's disappointing.

Even less melodramatic, we're now part of Britain's nation of shopkeepers. Our combined financial resources found us in a reasonably comfortable position, and so, looking for something we could work at together, the novelty of cooking full English breakfasts in somebody else's café having worn off, we bought the town's hardware business when its owner retired. Our surveyor's report confirmed what we'd expected; the shop doesn't appear to be built on a hell mouth either. Rather than inspiring excitement or fear, a small town hardware store constitutes a very popular asset in an era of edge-of-town DIY hypermarkets and internet shopping. The previous owners developed a sort of Aladdin's Cave of items from every genre of home improvement, but also a frankly disappointing catchphrase: "Sorry, we don't have any of those in stock; they'll be in on Friday.". There was a different catchphrase for Fridays. We've tried to be a bit more twenty-first century than that, but the customers still like the traditional brown coat and having screws and nails weighed out into brown paper bags. Brown's not really my colour, but I can bite the bullet.

The sun is already high enough to warm us as it shines through the dining room windows, even though it's only February, and the coffee warms us from the inside. But the sunshine also highlights the dust accumulating on every horizontal surface, which reminds me…..

"Meant to say, I had one of my regular dreams last night."

"Uh-huh? Bikes again?"

"No, the little-room-climbing-out-of-the-window one."

"Ah! The one where you wake up in panic."

Thirsty rather than panic stricken was my recent experience, I recalled, but I let it go. Actually, saying panic doesn't narrow it down much, although the bike dreams to which she refers tend to leave me in confusion rather than panic. Before Trish and I got together and discovered that we enjoyed walking together, ideally as far from the madding crowd as possible, I used to be a very enthusiastic cyclist. I discovered at an early date that I was never going to win prizes at it, but that does at least save having to dust a trophy cabinet. However, I could set a fair pace over long distances and would take part in endurance *sportifs*.

Walking hand in hand with Trish and nature, and filling brown paper bags with nails, leaves me with little time to get the bike out these days.

Except in my dreams.

There I'll be, powering effortlessly up some daunting hill, unstoppable, surging ahead of the pack. Or, frustratingly, just as frequently, I'll be turning up to enter a race in which I am a much fancied challenger, only to find that my bike is damaged, the tyres are flat, or I've forgotten to enter, or turned up after the race has started, or I don't have a bike at all and I have to run the race on foot instead. In the dreams where I do actually take part, and I'm leading the event, I'll lose sight of the direction arrows, which have disappeared in the middle of a busy town and I'll be completely lost and alone and find myself cycling inside a deserted multi-storey office block, climbing staircases looking for a window to climb out of......More windows! I've never made a habit of climbing through windows during my waking hours.

Not a panic inducing dream then, but confusing and frustrating. I have never ever finished a bike ride in my dreams. Even once would be nice; don't have to be the winner. I'd be happy to settle for a podium place!

Unlike me, Trish doesn't often remember much about her dreams, but this morning she did and her account was full of detail, none of which appeared to make a lot of sense to either of us. Our town's business association had asked us if we could decorate the town with Christmas lights. It wasn't Christmas, but they just thought it would cheer everybody up. So there we were, attaching dozens of light-festooned Christmas trees to the front of the shops and houses that make up the High Street. As we worked our way up the street we met another group, also stringing lights onto the buildings, a group led by our former employer at the café. He was in a foul mood, possibly because we were all getting in each other's way, or possibly because we'd both left his employ at the same time to start our own business.

She never found out the reason for his bad mood because she was distracted by the sudden appearance of a dog that wandered onto the scene, trailing its lead and all on its own. Trish managed to cajole the dog into coming to her and allowing her to take hold of its lead. The dog was pink, the lead a clashing bright green.

"A pink dog, eh? Where did you get that from? You don't even like dogs."

"True. Although the pink ones are probably okay," she grinned.

"Fair point; just don't eat a whole one. Talking of which, breakfast in Marlow could become lunch in Marlow if we don't get a move on."

"They call that Brunch, dear."

"Yes, very witty. Well whatever it turns out to be, I need to pop into the shop on the way, to pick up a sack of sunflower seeds for the birds. The forecast says that The Beast from the East is coming and our feathered friends are going to need some food. Can't have 'em dropping dead in the hedges. I might swipe a couple of dusters out of stock too."

"You reckless devil!" I hear her call back as she heads up the stairs to the bathroom.

I park the car outside the shop while I run in and collect the stuff that I need, then set the alarm and go through the elaborate door locking process again as I leave. I turn and reach for the car door handle. Something on the periphery of my field of vision distracts me. I look up at one of the old terraced houses on the other side of the road in time to see an indistinct face pull back quickly at an upstairs window, and the faded orange and yellow curtains cover the window and obscure my view.

"You okay, love?" She reacts to my getting in and then sitting motionless and apparently miles away instead of starting the car.

"Yeah, fine.....just thought I saw somebody watching me."

"That's just your vanity kicking in," she says playfully, and then adds, "Sitting here waiting for you, I've just remembered another bit of my dream. The High Street didn't end just down there." She points: "There was a sort of gate or archway or something and a whole lot more town on the other side of it. God knows where I got all that from."

"I've certainly never heard you mention that before."

"Mention what? An archway?"

"No; God. You said you were an atheist."

She punches me in the arm, like people do when their loved one cracks a joke that isn't funny, but not so hard that it stops me putting the car in first gear.

"Ouch! Right, Marlow then, or would you prefer a snack at the Rainbow Kennels?"

That earns me an exasperated half smile, but it's better than a punch in the arm.

Into The Gulf

Carla Adwell had definitely enjoyed better days out, even though the sun had shone cheerfully all day. The gentle sea breeze at Redcar beach didn't chill the air to the point where jackets were necessary, and her little boy, Stevie, had really had fun doing what four year olds do, digging in the sand and building a castle, with the occasional paddle in the still cold water. It was her husband that was giving her cause for disquiet. In spite of the fact that it had been his suggestion that he took a day off work and they did something together as a family, he didn't seem to be enjoying himself very much. And she wasn't sure that they were really very together as a family. He didn't seem to be his usual self, in fact he hadn't for a while, truth be told. What worried Carla was that she had experienced this behaviour before. Instead of their usual walking hand in hand, his hands remained in his pockets for much of the time, and then he would appear to realise this neglect and over compensate by making a big thing of putting his arm around her. The drive home was unusually free of conversation, except for his occasional comments about the news broadcast on the car radio.

It was the spring of 1991 and the Gulf War was getting to the point where the opposing sides were formalising the requirements for a ceasefire. The war had involved the better part of two million soldiers from thirty countries, said to be engaged in a fight for the freedom of the oil-rich country of Kuwait. The juxtaposition of the words "freedom" and "oil-rich" always brought out the best in the world's cynics. Well over eight thousand of the combatants would never get to hear about the details of the ceasefire, having already lost their lives in six weeks of military action.

Carla was hearing all about it though, whether she liked it or not. Back at home, as she unpacked the picnic cool-box in the kitchen, her husband was leaning on the kitchen door frame, reading from his damn newspaper. He did like his statistics and the editorial article he was perusing had plenty, but she was only half listening to what he said.

"….and listen to this. There's this war historian who says that Saudi Arabian society was upset by soldiers turning up from all over the world because it meant they got to see women wearing trousers and driving motor vehicles. Bloody hell! "As much as we appreciate your help beating Saddam Hussein, we can't be giving women too much freedom, now can we?" Still in the Dark Ages…"

The phone rings in the living room and he interrupts his diatribe to go and answer it. Carla couldn't help but notice his reaction to the sound; almost fearful, almost dropping the paper. From the living room came the muffled tones of his conversation, even quieter than the distance from the kitchen to the living room would justify. It didn't sound like a friendly chat and Carla's curiosity took her through to find out what was happening.

"…..alright. I'll think of something." And the receiver was hastily returned to its cradle.

"Who was that?" Carla asked, noticing her husband's face was suddenly drained of colour.

"Er....my brother....his car's broken down. Well, he's got a flat tyre, but he can't seem to get the wheel nuts off. You know what he's like." His hand is shaking as reaches for the car keys.

Carla isn't buying this. "Your brother phones with a flat tyre and you whisper about it? Look at yourself! Your face is white, your hands are shaking!" Her voice is raised now in frustration and a rapidly growing anger. "Who was that really?"

He just stares at her for a moment, and then turns to the front door with "I'm sorry, but I have to go and help somebody,..... a friend. I'll explain when I get back".

He's out of the door and into the car before she can stop him, and five seconds later the car moves off at speed. He always insisted on reversing the car up to their small terraced house in the cul-de-sac where they lived; joked it was his inner getaway driver manifesting itself. Not so funny now.

Carla stood motionless, trying to contain the panic and tears that were so close to the surface, until she was interrupted by the voice of Stevie who, throughout all this, had been quietly playing on the floor with his Lego bricks, making something that could've been a spaceship or it could've been a car transporter.

"Where's Daddy gone? He was very fast."

"Oh, he said he had to help Uncle Phil with his car. He's broken down somewhere. I don't suppose he'll be long." That seemed to be received as a satisfactory explanation and Stevie carried on with his construction, until his mother got down on the floor with him and gave him an extra long hug.

Nearly three hours later she heard the familiar sound of a car engaging reverse gear and the transmission whine as it came backwards down the road. The cat's ears twitched and its head lifted. Even the cat had learned the sound of a car reversing.

Stevie had long since been put to bed and Carla had had a restless evening. She'd tried to watch a bit of television. Channel Four was showing Monty Python's Life of Brian for the first time. It was something they'd both been looking forward to seeing and she gave it a try. But her laughter was forced and, unable to really concentrate, she switched it off. It was something they'd wanted to laugh at together and she felt a very long way from together. Or laughing.

"So…..how's your….. Friend?" Again, the response is a long stare. He fumbles the car keys from hand to hand, until he realises that this is becoming irritating and drops them onto a side table.

"This friend; what's her name? Oh come on! Don't keep lying to me; I can tell by your face I'm in the right ballpark."

His shoulders sag as he resigns himself to the fact that any attempt to hide the truth is now pointless.
"Does the name matter? Look…"

"It does to me, just this once. After this she'll just be referred to as The Bitch!"

"It's Yvonne, and she's not…"

"I don't want to know what you think she is or isn't, but I do want to know what the fuck she's doing in your life? How could you? You promised me four years ago that it wouldn't happen again.......Don't fucking touch me!" She screams this as he reaches out to put a hand on her shoulder, and he backs away realising that any moves to comfort her would be ill considered and in poor taste right now.

Carla turns her back on him, facing the window and hugging herself tightly.

"And there you were, banging on about Saudi men. You... pontificate about women's rights. What about mine, eh? Clearly some other woman's rights are a damned sight more important than mine....And what about Stevie's rights? What about our son?" She turns to shout this in his face, bursts into sobbing and then storms from the room and up the stairs, leaving her miserable partner standing there, speechless.

After about ten minutes she returns. Her face is red and her eyelids are swollen from crying. He looks up from the armchair he'd moved to.

"I've just been looking at our beautiful son......maybe it would've been better if you'd gone last time, but I really believed you were sorry."

"I was...."

"Why did you have to go out tonight? Planning your getaway?"

"No! Yvonne, er, she called to say she'd taken a load of paracetamols......."

"Ha! Enough to kill herself I hope, or at least kill her liver? Give me some ray of hope."

"No, it takes quite a lot to do any lasting damage, maybe about….."

"Please spare me the statistics on drug overdoses. So why are you back?"

"I told you I'd come back. I left her with a friend who was taking her to A and E to get checked out. She wasn't very happy about that."

"Oh shame! But suddenly I find me and The Bitch have something in common; two women whose evenings have been ruined by you! I need a fucking drink to celebrate," and she heads off to the kitchen returning with a glass with well over a double whisky in it. "Didn't get you one in case you're driving again tonight."

"I wasn't planning to."

"Well I don't think that's entirely up to you now, is it?"

"What are you saying?"

"I'm saying I don't think I want to live like this any more, living like a fucking doormat, somebody you can just walk over while you enjoy some secret life with somebody else. And I suppose she's younger and prettier than me…."

"No, actually she's older and…."

"Oh great! Now I get dumped for an older woman. Priceless!"

"I didn't say I was dumping you…."

"No, you bastard! You didn't say anything! Just sneaking around as usual, soaking up the flattery. Just keep me in the dark, where you want me. I'll say it again: I don't want to live like this. I've had enough of your lies….."

"I don't want to live like this either, it's….."

"It's what? Not your thing being happy with your wife and the son we created together? Rather be with somebody who isn't too tired for great, earth shattering sex every night?"

She drains the glass and goes back for a refill.

"Tell you what. I'm going to bed with this glass of whisky; you can always trust a good old, reliable glass of whisky. You can stay there in that chair, or drive to A and E or wherever. I don't care, I really don't. But take some time to think about what stuff in this house is valuable to you, because tomorrow you can box it up and take it away."

She leaves the room again, but turns in the doorway:

"What did I do wrong, eh? I did nothing but love you, Chris. Nothing! Just go to hell!"

DIY

"Right, Barbara. These shelves won't stack themselves. You choose: the electrical stuff or tins of paint?"

"Oh the electrics, definitely. My back won't stand lifting all them heavy five litre things. Not as young as I used to be, Mr A!"

"I'm no spring chicken either, but I did say you could choose. And not so much of the Mr A. It's Chris to you. Mr A makes me sound like "Typical Man in a magazine survey"; Mr A drives six point four miles to work, has two cats and rarely wears a hat."

"You don't drive six point four miles to work. You only live round the corner."

"…..Never mind, Barbara. Suppose we'd better get stuck in then."

We'd sort of inherited Barbara when we took the business over, the previous owners having employed her for at least a couple of decades. So she knew the shop, the customers and the products inside out; definitely an asset worth keeping.

"But I'm no good with all these computers and laptops and whatnot, Mr A. I miss writing everything down. I knew where I was with the little notebooks, but these days…..."

I had to admit that I wasn't much good with a computer either, but fortunately Trisha was and while we labourers stacked the shelves she was hard at work sorting out the invoices for the paint we'd just received and updating prices on our website. Trisha, who hated the full version of her name, insisted on taking care of the marketing and advertising;

"I daren't leave it to you. You'd have banners in the window saying "Let us do your nails" or "Everybody needs a good screw"."

"I was only kidding about that. Mind, if you're not busy when we get home….."

Trish came out of the office, partly to get a rest from looking at the computer screen for most of the morning and partly because it was her turn to make the tea.

"Tea's up," she said, handing out the cups, putting aside one for the fourth member of the team who was at that moment serving a customer.

"Thanks, Mrs..er Trisha." I pretend not to notice the sheepish look.

James comes back for his tea after the customer leaves.

"That's almost cleared us out of draught excluders. This Beast from the East is definitely good for business."

"Should be more in this afternoon's delivery, James. That and fleece for covering plants. And sharpened stakes for the Great Vampire Invasion."

He looks blankly at me. Or perhaps judgmentally.

Trish isn't a fan of cold weather though: "But can we go somewhere warmer for our holiday this year, Chris? As in, not skiing!"

"Fair enough. I hear Bognor Regis can be very pleasant in July. Weekend there?"
She makes as if to throw her tea at me.

"I was thinking of somewhere a little more Mediterranean than that, you clown. If you want to go to Bognor I'm sure James would be happy to take me to the South of France."
James blushes. He's only seventeen and works with us on Saturdays and occasional days fitted in around his A Levels. He's a bright lad.

I've always liked Trisha's sense of humour. Well I assume she was joking. She's always said she prefers older men, fortunately for me.

On the subject of holidays, there is a place in a Mediterranean country I've always wanted to take Trisha to see, a place I know really well; except that it doesn't exist. I know I'm making no sense here; bear with me. In my enthusiastic cycling days I had a few holidays on the Ionian island of Lefkada and spent many long days on its roads and trails. But the place I want to take my wife to see exists exclusively in my dreams, dreams in which we hire a couple of mountain bikes and I take her up this long winding hill climb to show her the most fantastic mountain and beach panorama. Our final destination is a little fishing port, a typical picture postcard Greek scene with blue and white buildings, busy tavernas, tourist cruisers and fishing boats being readied for the off, or bringing in the day's catch. Typically in the dream world, we never ever get there, but I'm utterly convinced this place is real.

Until I wake up, and then I know it isn't. I've even resorted to looking at a map of Lefkada, poring over every contour and coastal habitation for something that might be the inspiration for the place of my dreams. There isn't anything.

I stand with my cup of tea, looking out of the front window of the shop, watching passers-by bracing themselves against the bitterly cold east wind.

And then I look up at the first floor windows of the terrace opposite and realise that I can't see the faded orange and yellow curtains that I'd seen on that morning when we drove to Marlow. To be honest, I'm not sure I can even find the window.

The Joy Of Shopping

We've always agreed, Trisha and I, in the old adage that we should work to live, not live to work, not to let the tail wag the dog. I'm sure other clichés on the subject of work-life balance are available. Even so, running your own business is rarely a nine to five job, and it's difficult to find the time for the mundane things of life, never mind trips to exotic locations like Bognor Regis and the South of France.

Today was shaping up as a day to enjoy life not work, and it was a pleasant surprise to be strolling along, with no great urgency, humming to myself the tune of "No Particular Place To Go", through an old fashioned shopping arcade, an emporium, the sort of place that stands apart from all the ubiquitous chain stores that every town or city has. I had a sudden reminder of our brown coats and brown paper bags. It's like a trip back in time, with good, attentive and well informed service. Whether it's artisan bread or cheese or jewellery or Swiss knives or rare single malt whisky you might be looking for, this looked to me like the ideal location to be in.

And then suddenly I find myself looking through the window of a shop that sells model cars. Now this is something that's right up my street. I notice in a display case near the till, that there are the familiar blue and yellow boxes of old Matchbox cars. I'm immediately taken back to my childhood in the late sixties, the prized objects of desire for my pocket money. How much were they then? A shilling and ninepence, a shilling and ten pence? What's that in new money? Everybody said that in 1971.... Less than ten pence, or new pence as we called them then, and for years afterwards. Wow! What can you buy for less than ten pence these days?

As I said, I'm not in a hurry, so I go into the shop for a closer look. The models and their boxes look like the ones I used to collect, but I'm disappointed to see that these are all reproductions, all newly minted sixtieth anniversary editions, specially made for collectors,

The proprietor of the shop notices me looking, folds his newspaper and comes over to speak to me. Did I mention the good old fashioned service to be found in this arcade? It seems that this particular shop keeper hadn't got the memo.

"You gonna buy something or just stand there gawping?" That certainly helped to reinforce the idea that bad manners aren't exclusive to the much maligned "youth of today". James would never speak to a customer like that. This man looked old enough to be my father, and I'm fifty eight.

I decide not to retaliate and instead, I make allowances for his advanced age
.

"No, sorry, I was just looking. I thought these were genuine models, but they're just reproductions, so I'll give them a miss, if you don't mind."

"What do you mean, not genuine models? Of course they're genuine models. They're just new genuine models, not old genuine models." He seemed to find this funny, but when his cackling laughter had subsided he pointed at the door, hostility replacing humour as if somebody had thrown a switch.

"If you're not buying, you can get out. Go on; go forth and multiply!!"

At his use of this rather unsavoury Biblical metaphor I was so surprised, I just stood there looking at him.

"Go on. On yer bike! I know you've got one."

What? I've never seen him before, but the best I could come back with was, "Well I can see why I'm the only customer in the place."

"You're not a customer. You haven't bought anything!" Again, hilarious, but I turned and left before he could come up with any more gems from his own peculiar sales and marketing techniques.

My enthusiasm for shopping, never strong at the best of times, was very much on the wane and I decided to head for home, and I made my way out of the doors of the arcade onto the main streets. I had no idea where I was, none of the buildings looked familiar. What was happening? No need to stress. Probably I'd come out of a different door to the one I'd entered; easily done. So I retraced my steps through the arcade, noticing as I did so that the model shop was now full of people, the old man looking like he was treating them with a courtesy that had been very absent from my encounter with him. Not my problem.

My problem was that the streets at the other exit looked exactly the same as the ones at the first one I'd used. Nobody else seemed very bothered, or appeared to share my disquiet; just a normal, busy shopping day. I consider myself to have a generally good sense of direction, but right now, I don't have a clue where I am, never mind where I'm going.

Maybe if I sit down with a cup of coffee I can pull myself together and figure it all out. What did he mean about the bike? Never mind. These days, every town has a Costa or a Starbucks, doesn't it? I don't take long to find one and join the queue to get myself a drink. When it's finally my turn to order, I look up at the extensive drinks menu, and then the uniformed barista turns to face me.

It's the old man from the model shop!

"You gonna buy something or just stand there gawping?" His cackle is loud behind me as I turn to flee the shop. "Don't forget this!" I stop and turn again, and in his outstretched hand is a brown paper bag. I take it from him, with some apprehension. It's a bag of four inch nails. What the hell is going on?

"Need any help crucifying yourself?" he asks me, once again all traces of his smile gone. Dropping the bag I run outside and I manage to stifle the rising panic long enough to ask a passer-by, "Excuse me, but where is this?"

He looked at me as if I was mad. Couldn't really argue with him right then. "You're outside Costa, mate."

"No. I mean what town?" Again, the look.

"Ain't a town, pal. Leeds is a city." A bit of civic pride there.

"Leeds?!"

What the fuck am I doing in Leeds? I live in Oxfordshire. Somehow I've taken myself to Leeds for the day. It's the best part of two hundred miles from home. Did I drive here? My car must be parked somewhere.

My recent informant said Leeds, and I don't really know my way around Leeds city centre. But these streets are all long curves, which reminds me of Bath. I don't know Bath well either, but I know it from photographs. Isn't it called the Royal Crescent, the famous curved street? Yes, that's it. Well these streets are like that, only a bit shabbier and full of shops.

My annoyingly futile attempts to find a way out of this place lead me to an alley that suggests a route to the next street, but I find myself in an old residential area, with no sign of anything leading to a car park. At this point it belatedly occurs to me to wonder where Trisha is. It seems unlikely I would have gone all the way to Leeds without her. Maybe she's wandering around the shops wondering where I am. "Wandering and wondering," I mutter to myself as I take my phone out. No signal. Shit! Then I notice a movement in the street; up at a window, a hand pulls back a faded orange and yellow curtain.

I suddenly realise where Trisha is; she's in bed beside me, propped up on one elbow and looking at me.

"You alright Chris? Lots of rapid eye movement going on there."

"Yeah, I guess. It was a Leeds dream again. Why is it always Leeds? And there was a particularly unpleasant old man as well. That's new."

And why are there always curtains? And why have I seen them in real life?

What's Up, Doc?

I used to enjoy my insomnia. Sounds a bit possessive, doesn't it? My mate, insomnia; we go back a long way. Yes, I know going without sleep isn't good for you and that a good night's sleep does wonders for whatever processes make our minds and bodies function the way they ideally should. From time to time I've resorted to taking sleeping tablets to try and get the proverbial eight hours, but I found I still woke up in the middle of the night and then felt most tired when it was time to get up. Complete waste of time, but at least that means that there's little chance of me getting addicted to them.

But then I found that I didn't want to go to sleep at all. That's how much these dreams were bothering me. Well, not so much the dreams, but this curtain motif that not only kept cropping up in the dreams, but I was convinced was spilling over into my real life.

Surely though, it was much more likely that I was imagining the whole curtain thing. It's not as if orange and yellow are rare colours. I mean every rainbow has them. There must be more than just the one pair of curtains with that pattern and colour combination. And the dreams weren't exactly nightmares either. I'm sure lots of people dream about getting lost, or travelling to destinations and never reaching them. Could be worse I suppose. I could be publicly speaking with no trousers on. I find it helps me, if I employ that sort of flippancy, to get a sense of proportion. "Don't make such a fuss; there's always somebody worse off," I tell myself, as well as other hackneyed expressions intended to minimise the importance of personal crises. "First World problems"; that's another one.

Obviously taking pills to keep myself awake would be even worse for me, and definitely for those who would have to put up with me, than the ones designed to help me sleep. Likewise glugging pints of Red Bull. Then just as I'd bigged my devil-may-care routine up to opening night standards, something happened which sent the spiders of fear crawling up and down my spine.

At the hardware store we take in dry cleaning. It's not a massive earner any more, what with so many home washable fabrics in our lives now, but it's a useful service for the community and it gets people into the shop. Needs must. The garments are collected by a van on Thursday and they come back the following Tuesday.

One Thursday morning I was getting that week's collection ready for the van driver when I noticed in one of the plastic bags some orange and yellow floral fabric. The hair stood up on the back of my neck.

"Barbara." That didn't come out much above a hoarse whisper the first time. Take two: "Barbara, when did these curtains come in?"

"Oh, those grubby things. Yesterday afternoon, just after you'd left."

Trying to sound a lot more casual than I felt, I said, "They don't look as if they'd survive the cleaning process.

I hope whoever left them isn't expecting too much."

"Serve him right if they fall apart. Miserable old goat. Couldn't have been ruder if he tried."

"What do you mean, rude? Who was it?"

"Old feller; told me he was in a hurry and didn't have time to hang around waiting for me to stop gawping out of the window. Cheeky bugger! I was sorting out something that had fallen down in the window display when he came in."

"What did he look like?"

"Ancient, scrawny old thing, he was. Didn't think retired people needed to rush about any more. I know I certainly won't be doin' any of that! Can't wait to put me feet up, I can't."

Back at home that evening: "Something's bugging you, Chris. I can tell."

"I don't know, Trish. Maybe I'm just being silly, or working too hard, as they say."

"We're all working too hard…you slave driver."

"I know, and I appreciate all of you. It was just an expression. I didn't mean…….look; it's these dreams I keep having. I think I'm starting to see the same things when I'm awake," and I told her about the old man and the curtains. The buoyant, flippant side of me wanted to speculate if that was a book title that Hemingway had rejected, but to be honest I wasn't feeling completely light hearted about this situation.

"To be fair you do have a pretty vivid imagination, Chris. Well, except when it comes to birthday presents and planning meals." I managed a wry smile at this. There was, I had to admit, some truth in what she said; more than in the bit about me being a slave driver anyway.

"I know, and that's what I keep telling myself. I mean it's not like I can go to the police with "I keep seeing these flowery curtains and I think an old man is stalking me. And now he's bringing me his dry cleaning". "And where did this happen sir?" "Er, half in my dreams and half out."

"You know what they'd say don't you?"

"Yes, they'd tell me I've probably been working too hard. Or they'd go and check if the padded cell was vacant."

"Do police stations have padded cells? Look, seriously; while you've been trying to be funny, I've been Googling sleep disorders and dealing with bad dreams….."

"They're not so much bad as…."

"Shush a bit; there's a clinic that deals with them, the Milner Clinic, based in America."

"Hardly worth a Transatlantic flight…."

"With a branch in London. Might not even need to go there. Their website has a few suggestions. First of all, they suggest, go for a check-up with your own doctor. When was the last time you went for one of those? Your fiftieth birthday present, wasn't it?"

It was that long ago and, I had to admit, a present that was both imaginative and useful. It probably was about time I found out how my blood pressure and cholesterol levels were doing. I also have to admit, I've never actually taken the time to find out what cholesterol is, or does, or doesn't do. Wouldn't know it if I passed it in the street. I just know it's not supposed to be very high; a bungalow of a thing, not a skyscraper.

"You're right. I'll make an appointment. If I tell him about the dreams he'll probably refer me to a psychiatrist."

"And? Would that be such a bad thing?"

"You saying I'm crazy? Only about you, my dear."

Which is true.

"What else do they suggest, this, what is it? Milner Clinic?"

"Let's see; they say try discussing your symptoms, describing the dreams, rewriting the way the dreams finish."

"That's a good idea. I could punch that old man in the face!"

"You could smother him with the curtains!" Trisha read more. "Involve your partner to discuss your sleep patterns. Ooh, I wonder if they could cure you of fidgeting in the middle of the night. It would improve my sleep patterns. And it also suggests discussing your family history."

My family history. Now there's a Pandora's Box.

"And eventually, for the hardened dreamers, they can do something called polysomnography. No, it has nothing to do with the sex life of parrots. Do you want my help or not?"

I apologised and started reading over her shoulder that the Milner Clinic could provide a sleep situation for their patients with monitors for brain waves, blood pressure, heart rate and breathing, and film the whole thing.

"Sounds interesting. And expensive. Perhaps we'll start with the good old NHS. I'll make an appointment for that check-up."

The appointment was on the following Monday morning. Trisha opened up the shop and I walked the ten minutes or so up to the surgery. Doctor Peterson and I have known each other a long time. We are occasional hiking buddies too.

"Not so easy to keep the weight down when you get to our age, is it Chris?"

I instinctively pulled in my tummy.

"Don't do that. You can't fool me. I'm a doctor. I remember when you were built like a whippet. No, mate, you're basically alright. Blood pressure's fine, blood test results should be back in a week or so.…...So, want to tell me what's bothering you?"

I didn't mention that I had no idea what cholesterol was, but I told him what I'd told Trisha, accepting the risk that he probably knew more about locating a padded cell than the police did.

Back at the shop I decided to disregard patient-doctor confidentiality and filled Trisha in on the conversation at the surgery.

"So what did he suggest?"

"Ha! Among other things, perhaps I've been working too hard."

That's when I noticed the object standing on a shelf just outside our back office. It's a blue-white ceramic pot containing a miniature rose, a yellow rose.

"Where the hell did that come from?"

"The rose? It's Barbara's. An old man brought it in while you were at the doctor's. He said it was to say sorry for being so rude the other day."

Gateway To Hell

Surprisingly, I had a good night's sleep the next night. There was only so long I could stay awake thinking about what I'd seen before exhaustion rendered me unconscious. Trying to balance the rational, coincidence based explanation against the dread feeling that somebody was playing out some malevolent prank at my expense was getting me nowhere. I'd panicked when I heard about the old man who'd visited the shop, but, to be fair, I hadn't actually seen him. It could be somebody else entirely. No! It must be somebody else entirely. People don't turn up out of your dreams, do they?

When I said a good night's sleep, I did wake up at about two, having enjoyed a dreamless few hours, but needing a drink of water. Thirst quenched, I followed my routine of picking some music to listen to downstairs, something relaxing to get me back off to sleep. I almost went for Tangerine Dream's "Phaedra", but I wanted sleep, not a coma, so it was one of the Jacques Loussier Trio's Bach arrangements instead, familiar and pleasantly light.

Having tuned out very quickly somewhere in the opening Gavotte, I woke up feeling ready for anything. I took a few moments to check if I was really awake, not just dreaming about being awake. Result! Today is the day the dry cleaning comes back to the shop, and I suppose the old man could come back at any time too. I tried to imagine the elderly gentleman, as he'd been described to me, standing on a pair of steps, hanging his own curtains; that seemed unlikely.

The laundry's van dropped off at ten and I checked the items against the invoice. No curtains. The driver shrugged his shoulders. Promising him I wouldn't shoot the messenger, I phoned the dry cleaners and asked if they'd forgotten to load them.

"I'll check, mate." He frequently does that gag; waits to see if I'm going to respond with "No, I can still move my king" or similar, but I'm not in the mood today. "What's the ticket number?"

"Five-oh-seven." I nervously hummed the little bit of the Gavotte I could remember while I waited.

"Don't have a five-oh-seven, mate. Never came here. Funny that, cos we've got six and eight. Sure you haven't ripped it out of the book by mistake?"

That mental debate I was having last night about coincidence versus malevolence? Coincidence was starting to slip back in the running, with very long odds. I had the chilling feeling that I wasn't going to see the old man again, at least not during waking hours. Shit! It's only been a few days since I was thinking how good life was and here I am in need of.....well, what? Psychiatric help? Dream interpretation? An exorcist? Our morning coffee ritual will be ruined if my head starts spinning round and round.

Once again I'm starting to dread falling asleep, and once again, in the middle of the night I find myself in the version of Leeds that my subconscious has invented. This time there's no arcade, no terraced houses. I'm on the ring road in my car, looking at a green destination sign telling me I can take the A653 to Dewsbury or the A650 to Wakefield, or I can follow the blue rectangles to the various motorways leading north or west; in short, anywhere but south, and I want to go south. I want to go home, but my car has decided that it doesn't want me to go anywhere apparently. It has completely ceased to function. In fact it has completely changed function. It was an Audi A6; now it's a van.

Something breaks into this narrative and I actually manage to tell myself that this is just a dream, my car will be alright. Or I've started dreaming about dreaming, because it's not enough to wake me up and the next thing I know I'm on a railway platform about to board a train. I have no idea what the train's destination is, but I get jostled along with the other passengers and find myself practically pushed into a carriage. A railway guard is trying to keep some kind of order, but as he turns I'm shocked to see that it's him again, the old man, my nocturnal nemesis. Where did that ridiculous bit of alliteration come from? Makes him sound like a super-villain in a comic strip. I don't know why I should be shocked to see him again. The shocking thing is what he's wearing. It's not the uniform of a railway guard; it's a Nazi SS uniform.

In spite of my bafflement, mixed with horror, at his latest persona, I decide that maybe it's time I confronted this persistent blight on my life, but before I can say anything he smiles and stretches out an arm. I realise he is directing me to a seat. I'm not used to receiving any kind of courtesy from him, but I turn anyway to see where he is pointing and I am staggered to see my first wife, Carla, and my son, Stevie sitting there.

"Daddy," Stevie cries out, and he jumps up to give me a hug. I bend down to hug him back, noticing that Carla is not anywhere near as pleased to see me. Hugging Stevie was a reflex action, but then I'm trying to figure out how and why we are back together again, and, after a nudge in the back from my acquaintance in the Nazi uniform, all sitting on the same seat together. I've spent nearly thirty years away from Carla; all that effort and I'm back at square one.

"I'm really looking forward to seeing Grandma again, Daddy. Are you?"

I turn and look blankly at Carla. She gives me an exasperated grimace in return.

"Surely you remember. We have some unfinished business with my mother."

Of course I don't remember, but I reckon that I'll find out sooner or later. It turns out to be quite soon; before the train moves off, the door opens again and in walks the aforementioned mother-in-law. Or I suppose it's ex mother-in-law. In fact, just to add to my confusion, I know she died about five years ago, but there she is, as large as life.

In happier times, that is, back in the days when Carla and I appeared to be a permanent and contented couple, I was permitted to call her mother Maggie. ("I think he's good for you, dear. He's got a lovely dark brown voice"…. I'm always happy to take a compliment, but this did seem a strange basis for a character assessment.) I wasn't going to risk that today.

"Er….Margaret. Good to see you," I lied.

"Is it? Really?" She drew herself up to her full five feet five in heels. "Well in my opinion you have dealt treacherously with my daughter. I cannot countenance how she can tolerate sitting next to you!"

She had always had an uncanny flair for sounding like an Old Testament prophet condemning the wanton ways of the Israelite nation.

"Mother! Not now, please. Stevie doesn't need to hear this." I didn't need to hear it either. Well perhaps I did, to be fair, but I didn't want to, and besides this, my attention was distracted by watching the guard, who appeared to be loving every bit of my discomfort.

Somehow Margaret managed to seat herself in a position where she could avoid looking at me, and the train then started to move. I had no idea where we were headed, never mind why. The view of the Leeds suburbs soon became a view of the Yorkshire Dales, a part of Britain that I used to be very familiar with. I would have expected the train to continue beyond Skipton and Settle to the open countryside leading to the spectacular Ribblehead Viaduct. So why were we travelling through dense forest? And why was even the view of that gradually disappearing as the windows of our carriage seemed to recede until they were just narrow, barred slits near the ceiling? The carriage was becoming very crowded, overcrowded. This is ridiculous; surely there must be some legal limit to how many people you can carry on a train. Even cattle would be transported better than this. Now we had gone beyond the point of infringing personal space. We were packed so tightly we were almost having to take it in turns to breathe.

I could hear Stevie crying, but couldn't do anything to help him as the crush of bodies prevented me from moving, but I could just see Carla with her arms round him, and she too was in tears. Margaret was.... I had no idea where Margaret was. I suddenly found myself outside the packed carriage, witnessing what was happening from a different perspective. I was looking down on the train, in time to see it slow down and pass under an archway which bore three words:

ARBEIT MACHT FREI

The archway and the words are so infamous, deeply etched into our modern historical landscape; lying, deceitful words that spelt anything but freedom for the thousands that were unlucky enough to pass beneath them.

I know enough of twentieth century history to recognise this place. This is Auschwitz. What kind of railway line goes from Leeds to Auschwitz? What the hell are we doing at Auschwitz? This is terrifying. I've always had a fascination with this worst example of human cruelty and I have sat with morbid horror through Schindler's List or Escape From Sobibor, but I never imagined, in my wildest dreams that I would be one of the victims of the Third Reich's Final Solution.

I watch, disbelieving, as my family is marched off the train, and the familiar, cruel, grinning face of the train guard looks up at me, points at Carla, Stevie and Margaret and then at the smoking chimney behind him. He passes his finger under his throat in the universal gesture for death, then points at me and repeats the gesture. I feel hands grabbing me, pulling on my shoulders, and I am overwhelmed with the fear of my own certain death.

Trisha is shaking me: "Chris! For God's sake! What the hell is going on? It's four o' clock in the bloody morning."

"I'm sorry; really bad dream. A nightmare." One of my wildest dreams.

"Chris, this is getting ridiculous. Everybody has dreams."

"Yeah, s'pose so…...look, try to get back to sleep, love. I'm sorry."

She turns away, obviously disgruntled at this latest bit of melodrama ruining a good night's sleep.

"What was it about this time?"

"I was on a train with Carla and little Stevie, and Carla's mother. No idea where we were supposed to be going, but we all finished up at Auschwitz."

She turns back and props herself up on her elbow, looking slightly more sympathetic.

"You've been crying. What on earth goes on inside your head? That's horrible."

"It was horrible. There was this Nazi guard on the train and he was pointing at the chimney. I took that to mean that was where we were all going. That's when I woke up."

"But you've had these dreams of imminent death before, haven't you? Sometimes it's aliens and the end of the world."

"Yes, you're right. But the guard was that old man I keep seeing, y'know? The one that's been to the shop?"

"Now hang on. You haven't actually seen him in the shop; you've only been told about him. You can't be certain it's the same guy."

I was quiet for a moment while I thought about this.

"Fair enough, I guess." Then more emphatically, "But what if….I mean….no, I know it wouldn't stand up in court, so to speak…..."

"Look love, I know this is bothering you, but seeing curtains and pots of roses, I don't know…Maybe the doctor was right. Maybe you should have a chat with somebody else."

"You mean a psychiatrist? He'll probably just tell me it's all in my mind." Finally I feel a bit like laughing, "I guess that's what he does for a living, eh? "It's my professional opinion Mr Adwell, that you are as nutty as a fruit cake"."

"I could tell you that, for nothing! Look, can we get another couple of hours and we'll talk about it in the morning? I mean the proper morning, the one where most people get up, not this one where no sane person does, only you."

At breakfast Trisha comes up with another idea:

"I've thought of something. If you don't fancy a shrink, how about having a chat with my friend Melanie? You know who I mean?"

I knew who she meant: her best friend; tall, slim, almost white-blonde, and, I've always thought, slightly away with the fairies. And I remembered that she was into reading meaning into dreams, or some such mumbo jumbo.

"Of course I know who you mean. Your ditsy blonde who's into all the dream interpretation mumbo jumbo."

"That's a bit rich, coming from someone that thinks he keeps seeing magical plant pots."

"They're not….oh, alright. What's the plan then? Get a friend to tell me I'm mad instead of paying for a shrink?

"I get the impression Mel thinks you're mad anyway, darling! But she was asking about you the other day; said she thought you looked a bit tired and stressed last time she saw you and wondered if something was bothering you. No, just tell her what sort of things you dream about and perhaps you'll have a better idea of what's behind it all. I'm sure she'd love….well, she'd love the attention. What I mean is, try to look as if you're taking her seriously and she'll be in her element."

"I haven't seen her for ages! Either I've been looking rough for longer than I thought or she's been stalking me. Mind, it's not a bad idea. Anyway, what have I got to lose? And it'll be cheaper than going to a psychiatrist."

"Well there is that, Mr Cheapskate. Just fork out for a good bottle of red and she'll be happy."

"I think I might just tell her about the dreams though, and not all the, how should I put it? The extras."

Trisha phones Melanie from work later that morning.

"Right, so Mel's up for that, and she made a very practical suggestion; why don't you email her some of your plots, as she put it, and that'll give her time to look up some info before we go."

"That is practical, for Mel." The look I get tells me my Brownie points account is well overdrawn.

"Chris, you're exasperating sometimes. Perhaps she'll just come to the conclusion that they're exactly the sort of dreams an ungrateful git deserves."

"Sorry, I like her really."

"I know you do, but possibly because she's a tall blonde. Makes a change from the medium sized brunette you've got at home."

"Ouch! I like looking at Ferraris, but I'm more than happy with the Audi."
Perhaps I could have worked on that analogy a bit longer before delivering it. It earned me another withering look;

"Well this Audi can't stand around here gassing all day; she has work to do, and so do you. I'm just glad we don't have a pick-up truck."

So we worked, but later, back at home I put together a list of my dream themes and pinged it over to Mel. I told her about the grotty little room with the feeling of threat, about the staircases and corridors, the frustrating bike rides and the fictitious holiday destination. I included the curtains and the roses, but only in the ones in the dreams, not the real world manifestations. Should I mention the family on the train and the extermination camp? Yeah, why not? That seemed enough to be going on with, and it would certainly cover what I could remember of my recent night-time dramas. If we needed a bit of light relief I could always add Trisha's pink dog into the mix.

It might be interesting to quiz Mel on her specialist subject. We'd known her for the best part of ten years, but

I had never really seen much of her other than her 'always game for a swift drink, always happy to water the plants if we went on holiday' persona. Trish had got to know her a year or so after the time of the double whammy on my car. At that point Trisha and I had just moved in together, the two of us and my cat, a fit and healthy tom, the scourge of the local mice. And then he went missing, and all our calling and searching and posters on lamp posts were in vain.

We missed our cat; not so much the gifts of half chewed mice, but his contented purring as we watched the television together, or the lump under the duvet that told us he'd disobeyed the instruction not to sleep on our bed.

Then one afternoon Trisha came home with a kitten. She had bumped into a woman putting a "Kittens: Free to a good home" ad in the newsagent's window. That was Melanie.

Trisha was invited round to her house to see the kittens and she and Mel have been friends ever since and the kitten has grown old and comfortable with us. It always surprised us that Melanie didn't keep any of the kittens for herself.

Gin 'n' Treachery

Yvonne Robinson was a happy woman. The man she was in love with was sleeping next to her and for once he would still be there in the morning when they woke up. For the last few months theirs had been a relationship of stolen moments, of clandestine meetings for a couple of hours in an afternoon, or indeed any time of day when their schedules and devious imaginations could find them a way to cover their tracks.

She'd loved having somebody in her life who made her feel special, and he was such a lovely man. It appeared that everybody liked him, but she felt privileged that she was the one that was the recipient of his intimate attentions. He made her feel loved, and she hadn't felt like that for a long time.

That had been part of the problem up until now really. All those loving feelings, and then he left her on a high, going straight back home to his wife, leaving Yvonne lonely with just the telly and the remnants of the wine they'd shared for company. And she was becoming really fed up with all the sneaking around. It was obvious his marriage was over. Why else would he keep spending so much time with her and, as the months went by, expressing his love for her with increasing intensity? And she knew this wasn't the first time he'd strayed away from his wife, because he'd told her. She'd appreciated his honesty, although she had to admit the irony, seeing as he was being very dishonest at home.

He didn't talk about his wife and his little boy much; probably felt too guilty being reminded of them and would rather just live in the moment. But Yvonne was getting a little bit fed up with only having moments. She was beginning to wonder if the conversations they'd had about running away together were just fantasy. It was becoming obvious that the one about living on a houseboat in the South of France definitely was. That was one of her ideas that he had responded rather vaguely to.

He always became a little bit quiet and distant when she instigated this sort of subject, as if he worried that they didn't have the wherewithal to make their escape, or didn't even want to escape. It's not as if they didn't have secure jobs: he was the regional manager for the car hire company they both worked for and she ran the branch in Sunderland.

She wasn't stupid. She knew their salaries would be severely hit by the cost of his separation and divorce, especially if his wife was vindictive and obstructive. But, damn it, that one had her chance and it clearly wasn't working. Of course there was the little boy to think of, but other people seemed to manage alright, and the kid was young enough to get over it. Well kids adapt, don't they?

Yvonne had reached the point where she didn't really want to know about where he was or what he might be doing at the weekends. Sundays were the worst; long dull days without him, days when her imagination had too much empty time, thinking up what he might be doing at home. Correction: the recent Monday morning when he'd turned up early before work to make love with her was the worst. She could still smell the condom he'd used the night before.

"Well that's just great! A real passion killer!"

"I'm so sorry. I sneaked out early without time for a shower."

"Thanks a lot. It's bad enough thinking about you being with her all weekend, without this…this evidence of your bedroom activities."

"Look, I can't just stop having sex with her, can I? I think she's suspicious of me anyway."

"But Chris, she's going to have to find out sooner or later. I mean, isn't she? I mean, that's what we both want, isn't it?"

"Yeah, yeah, of course. But it's not easy trying to find the right time."

"No! It never is, is it?" She jumps out of bed and heads for the shower. "Better get ready for work. I've got a busy day at the office, and heaven forbid we should turn up in the same car!"

So ended their first row. Not exactly a blazing punch-up, but enough to cause her to phone her best friend Sheila, from whom she kept no secrets.

"The Fox after work? Six thirty-ish?"

Sheila was there already at six thirty, and already well into her first G'n'T. A nod to the barman produced another one for Yvonne and they took themselves over to a corner table for a bit of privacy.

"You're quite sure he's the one then? I mean you've been wrong a few times before, haven't you?"

"Cheeky mare! You know how to make me feel good about myself…..Yes, I love him, it's just, well, he says he loves me too, but sometimes I feel, oh I don't know….I don't want to just be his bit on the side. I mean, I'm nearly thirty. Clock's ticking. Know what I mean?"

"Only too well. With you there, Pet. But listen," said Sheila, getting into her stride now, "If he reckons his missus has already got her suspicions, well perhaps it's time to put the poor cow out of her misery. I mean he's not being fair to her either. If I was her I'd like to know where I stood, not be strung along with lies for months on end. Wouldn't you?"

Yvonne thought about this slightly twisted altruism.

"Suppose so. But I don't know what to do. I mean he's got a day off tomorrow and he's taking her and the kid out for the day. I'll be sitting in my office, trying not to think of them walking on the beach or wherever."

"Look, you stop smudging your mascara and I'll get a couple more of these," as she stands up, clinking the empty glasses together. "But you're getting the next round; being your love life consultant is costing me a fortune."

When Sheila comes back with the refills, she brings an idea.

"What you need is a catalyst. Is that the right word Something that causes a reaction? Give him a jolt, something to make him jump."

"What if he jumps the wrong way?"

"Yep! Gin certainly makes you pessimistic. Come on! At least you'll know one way or the other what his priorities are, won't you?"

Yvonne wasn't entirely convinced about Sheila's idea. It seemed a bit dramatic, a bit more than just rattling his cage. But when she got back to her flat, the phone rang. It was Chris, calling from a phone box on his way home after a late finish at head office.

"Yvonne, I'm really sorry about this morning. I'll think of some way out of this soon."

Whether it was listening to Sheila's black and white analysis of her situation or the effect of three double gin and tonics, the same old apology and the same old forecast sounded a bit lame and she reacted angrily.

"Well you'd better, because I don't think I can go on like this much longer. You know I love you, but I don't think I can waste much more of my time sharing you. So have a nice day tomorrow, but don't be too surprised if you hear from me at some point!"

She cut the call off then and ignored the phone twice when he tried to call back.

Perhaps Sheila's stunt would work, a stunt involving a paracetamol bottle and some homeopathic tablets.

Turning then to put her arms round Chris who was sleeping in bed beside her, she reflected that the plan had worked better than she could ever have expected. Her phone call to his house, telling him that she'd become so desperate that she'd taken an overdose, had him at her front door within an hour. He was all love and concern, and agitation; agitation because now the cat was well and truly out of the bag and amongst the pigeons. She knew he'd have to go home, but this time it would be to face the music. Sheila could be cruel, but brilliant.

The second part of the scheme was that Sheila would turn up and generously offer to take Yvonne to Accident and Emergency to prevent Chris's life from getting any more complicated than it was already rapidly becoming. Yvonne's role in all this was to look very unwell and distraught and make feeble gestures towards the empty pill bottle. She'd crunched up a few of the homeopathic tablets to achieve a white-powdered lip authenticity. To be honest, she could've done with a couple of real paracetamols; the stress of all this subterfuge was giving her a headache.

Sheila couldn't give any guarantee that her outrageous plan would work, but it had. Chris had turned up at her flat the next evening, looking somewhat sheepish, but promising he would stay the night this time instead of going home. He was no longer welcome back there. Yvonne had called in sick at work that day to give credibility to her overdose story and when Chris phoned her later at home she assured him that A & E hadn't needed to keep her in. He expressed real surprise that the quantity of tablets she'd ingested hadn't caused more damage.

"That's incredible. All those pills! I thought you would've at least wrecked your liver."

"I'm a tough old bird, but I'm sorry about all the drama. They told me I just need a few days' rest to get over it. How are things at your end…….?".

What Does It All Mean?

Melanie's husband Greg opened the door to me and Trisha on Saturday evening. I endured his usual hand mangling greeting while Trisha rubbed her face after Greg's clumsy kiss on both cheeks.

"Aha! You've come to consult the local witch I hear. Sure you wouldn't rather be down at the Rugby Club Quiz Night with me?"

"Tempting, Greg, but I think Mel's put a fair bit of work in on my behalf and I don't want to look ungrateful. But, hey, if you need to phone a friend….."

"What's the point, Chris? You don't know anything!"

"True, but at least it's stopped people asking me silly questions."

We could've kidded around like this for ages, but the Rugby Club wouldn't wait forever, and Trish and Mel were already rolling their eyes and tutting, so we relented.

Mel took us through to the kitchen-dining room, where their eight seater oak table was strewn with books and paper, evidence that she had indeed been working hard. She said that she liked to do her research the old fashioned way:

"Google's great, I know, but I've got a shelf full of books and I do know my way around them. Some of them are really old and valuable. They were passed on to me by an old friend who died recently. She really knew her stuff. My mentor, I suppose I'd call her." We decanted three glasses of the red we'd brought with us and arranged ourselves round the kitchen table.

"It's funny," said Mel, "The irony is that I hardly ever remember my own dreams. So it's nice to have so much detail to work with. I'm assuming these are real dreams and you're not just making it all up, or worse."

"Worse?"

"Yeah. I mean do you go creeping around stairs and corridors and climbing out of windows in real life?"

"Ha ha! No, Mel, my cat burgling days are well and truly behind me. But seriously, what is it with all the buildings and windows and stuff?"

"So let's do the buildings first. It's probably stating the obvious to say that they represent the constructions we make in our lives, but that's it."

"Fair enough, but if you start with the assumption that nothing is obvious to me, you can say what you like. I don't mean I'm thick. I mean it's your subject, not mine. I'm entirely in your hands, so to speak."

"He's not flirting with me, is he Trish?"

"Probably, although he's a reformed character these days. Or so he tells me."

"Well he would say that……"

"Hello! Still here!" I interrupted, looking from one to the other, hoping this was just light banter. Melanie had only a hint of a smile as she continued;

"Which brings us neatly back to buildings, the constructions. That could mean attitudes and beliefs that we've built over the years, either from our own experiences or from stuff that's been handed down; our family background, a bit of a mixture of nurture and nature you could say. And of course, we form our own habits and customs as we go along, don't we." Mel pauses to take another sip of red wine, which is definitely one of her habits and customs. She seemed to be working on the mere hint of smile too.

"But I always seem to be clambering in and out of these buildings. I get in and then I try to escape. What do you make of that?"

"The buildings could also be reflecting your current hopes and concerns, stuff that's worrying you perhaps. Or perhaps your history"

"I don't really worry about much these days, except the next VAT bill."

Trisha interrupts;

"What! We've come here because these dreams are really bothering you. You don't wake up sweating and shaking because of the VAT bill. Come on!"

"Fair enough, you're right." I look at Trisha, and then, "Should I tell her? Y'know, about the other stuff?"

This has got Mel's attention;

"Other stuff? What do you mean? What are you up to now?"

"What do you mean, "now"? You make it sound like I have a history of being up to something."

"Oh, I know you'll have something in your history. But come on; what other stuff?"

"What he means is he keeps seeing things from his dreams when he's awake. Or thinks he does!"

I can't help but notice the hint of scepticism, but something to balance my childlike belief is not a bad thing I suppose.

"Good grief! And I thought you were on my side. Look I know this sounds far-fetched, but I'm sure that some of the things I see in my dreams are popping up, no, popping up's a bit frivolous; but they're appearing and disappearing when I'm awake."

Mel's looking at me without saying anything. I start to feel a bit silly, slightly ganged-up on.

"See! I told you she'd think I was mad."

"Ah, but if you remember I said that Mel already thinks you're mad. This just confirms her suspicions."

"Okay then, let's get back on track, About these buildings; any thoughts about me climbing in and out of windows? We can get back to my paranoid daydreams later."

"Yes, we must," says Melanie, sounding reluctant to be getting back on track. "Windows then. First and foremost and fairly obviously; can I say obviously? Yes? Windows are for looking through, so that could refer to the way we see the world we live in, the way we perceive reality. But climbing in and out of them? We may be struggling to deal with inner feelings we want to escape from or perhaps how we feel about public opinion."

I know this isn't an exact science, but it's food for thought, although only an *amuse bouche* if you ask me.

"Hmm…..any ideas about the things in that little room I told you about, like the pot of roses, the cheesy ornaments and the curtains?"

"Well furnishings in a room suggest some aspect of the dreamer's personality…."

Trisha bursts out laughing: "This is why I don't let you pick the colours and stuff when we decorate."

"No, I'm just the grunt with the paint brush! But I can't figure out what yellow roses and orange and yellow curtains have got to do with my personality either. I mean apart from my generally sunny disposition, that is."

"Er, didn't you say they were faded curtains, Darling? Past their best?"

I glare at Trisha and gesture towards the plate with the pizza on it: "Have another piece; I know you won't talk with your mouth full!"

"I don't know about those specific items, Chris, but feeling threatened by someone or something in the next room is interesting. It could mean that some aspect of your personality is causing you a problem or even threatening you. Is there something bothering you? Something happening now or something that happened in the past?"

"Alright then, so we've got a building made of my achievements that I seem to spend my time trying to escape from, and I'm trying to get away from some aspect of myself that's threatening me. Sounds like I don't really like myself very much."

"Well is there something you've done that you don't like yourself for? Anything you're ashamed of?"

These questions are getting a bit challenging! Yes, I know there is, and Trisha knows there is, but I don't feel happy about sharing it with Melanie right now. Trisha steps in to divert the course of the conversation.

"Don't be too hard on him; it is only a dream."

"But it isn't, Trish. This is the other stuff that we were talking about. I keep seeing some of these things when I'm awake. Like the curtains, at least twice now. And the flowers. I mean they're very nice flowers. I like roses. But, roses and curtains? All seems a bit mundane. And there's this old man, and before you say anything, no, I haven't actually seen him, but I've heard about this old man…...he's kind of on the fringes of my life. It feels like I'm being watched!"

"An old man? You didn't mention him in your emails." Melanie looks somewhat agitated for a brief moment. "Can you remember what he looked like?"

"Looked old enough to be my father. A little wizened thing with a very mean sense of humour. I've seen him in several dreams; in a model shop, a coffee shop, on a train and at Auschwitz, for God's sake!"

"Do you think it could be him in the other room, behind that door?"

"I suppose that makes sense, but then you're saying that he's a part of my personality, that there is something about me that's, what, hunting me down, winding me up? And what does dreaming about an old man mean, if anything?"

"Not sure. I'll have to see what I can find out about him, what he's up to."

Melanie has a far-away expression on her face. Maybe she doesn't know how to answer this. Her books probably don't cover my situation, and I guess I'd be a bit puzzled if I were her, with me on one hand insisting that what I'm seeing is real, but getting the distinct feeling that my wife isn't too convinced about any of it. Objectively, dreams don't come true like this, so she tries for a rational explanation;

"But Chris, your life seems pretty stable now. Couldn't be rosier, is the impression I get. Dead jammy, if you ask me. I mean, you're in good health, good steady business, good steady wife," raising her glass in salute to Trisha, who responds with her glass, then realises it's got nothing in it and starts to uncork another bottle. "You don't appear to have any wasting diseases. The present looks good. So again, maybe there's something way back in your past that nags away at you."

She does seem hell-bent on digging into my past. Okay then….. I realised that neither Trisha or I had ever told Melanie much about my life before we met her. Trisha knew that I didn't really like talking about it and she had kept that confidence. But perhaps letting her know what happened next might be relevant. It was, after all, one of the things that nagged away at me.

Tripped Up

Yvonne Robinson was no longer a happy woman. Just lately she was hardly seeing any more of Chris than she was when he was with his wife. Even when he was there, he often seemed preoccupied. It's not like he wanted to turn back the clock; well she didn't think so anyway.

Being realistic, she hadn't expected Carla to be happy about Chris leaving, although she did chuck him out. It bothered her a bit, that. Would he have jumped if he hadn't been pushed? Never mind! He was with her now, but what looked like plain vindictiveness on his ex's part was really taking the shine off things.

"Carla says she doesn't want you spending any time with Stevie. Not one second, she says."

"What! Can she say that? Legally, I mean?"

"I don't know, but I don't really want to rock the boat with her. Things are hard enough and I don't want Stevie caught up in the middle of a war. We'll just have to put up with it for a while and hope things improve soon. Don't look like that!"

Yvonne responds with a sulky, "Yeah, we'll just see how it goes….."

And the way it went was that Chris spent a large part of his time most weekends with his son and Yvonne was back to being on her own, wondering what he was doing. It wasn't much better than the way it had been before, and it was just going on for, well, for months now, and Chris didn't seem to be doing anything to change things. She loved him, but he could be so infuriatingly.......submissive when it came to dealing with Carla, when he should be standing up for his rights. She knew the truth that a little boy needs his dad and it was impossible to argue against that, but still, she felt like she was being shut out, especially when Chris came back home an hour late one evening.

"Problem?"

"No, sorry I'm late. I needed to talk about some stuff with Carla." Yvonne had made a move to hug Chris, but she pulled back sharply.

"How come I can smell her perfume on you? Must've been quite a cosy chat!"

"Look, she just got a bit overwhelmed with everything that's going on and, well, she started crying on my shoulder. She started it."

"Started what, for God's sake?"

"Nothing! Nothing happened. She was just upset about the whole divorce thing, that's all. And then she realised what she was doing and backed off…."

"Oh she realised what she was doing alright! Oldest trick in the book!"

"What's that supposed to mean?"

"Women are cunning, that's all, and men are so gullible. Crying on your shoulder's just the first step to luring you back."

"That's not how it looked to me."

"Like I said, cunning. I can see I'm going to have to be even more cunning than I was last…..I mean, than she is."

"Even more cunning than you were last….. what? Than last time? What are you saying?"

"I meant, than her recent attempt to fool you."

"No you didn't. You were going to say "even more cunning than last time". What's that supposed to mean? Which last time? Are you talking about the night you took all those pills? Jesus! You are, aren't you?"

"Chris, you know I'd do anything for you. I love you."

"I know you do, but what did you mean? It's the paracetamol episode, isn't it? I would have said taking an overdose of pills is desperate, not cunning."

"I was desperate!"

"How come you were back home the next day? That many pills would have done you serious damage. Unless you faked the whole thing."

"How dare you!"

"Did you even go to hospital?"

"Of course I went to the bloody hospital! Sheila took me, if you remember."

"Did she now? Sheila. Your best mate. Another cunning woman! You're right about one thing though; I am gullible, falling for your con trick. That whole pill thing was a hoax, wasn't it? That was unforgivably deceitful."

"Deceitful? That's a bit fucking rich! We were having an affair. You were cheating on your wife!"

"Oh! And I suppose all's fair blah blah blah. I thought we were at least being honest with each other. I don't know which is worse: attempting suicide to get somebody's attention or pretending to. You didn't have to con me into being with you."

"Really? You kept telling me your marriage was over, but I could've grown old and grey waiting for you to do something about it. I had to do something."

"You admit it then? You faked the whole thing. There's me, trying to find a way to let her down gently……."

"Yeah, right! Chris, the caring adulterer. If you care so much why don't you just go back? Let her cry on your other bloody shoulder as well."

"Because I don't want to go back. Me and Carla are finished. But I have to say, right this minute, I'm not sure I want to be here with you either. I don't like being conned. I think I need some air. See you later maybe, but don't wait up."

"Chris! Chris?"

Mumbo-Jumbo

"So if you didn't go back to your wife, where did you go?"

"Just drove around feeling really pissed off with Yvonne and life in general, but eventually I asked my brother, Phil, if I could doss down in his spare room for a couple of days, just to give myself some thinking space. This was in the good old days before we could exist without a mobile phone, before we could be nagged with calls and texts and emails every hour, day and night."

"I know that Yvonne would have tried to get hold of you. Sorry. I mean, I assume she did."

"Yes, messages everywhere. And I wasn't trying to hurt her, but I just needed time to sort my priorities out. I mean I loved her, in spite of the whole pill bottle fiasco, but I needed to have regular time for my son in my life without an atmosphere brewing all the time. So I didn't hurry back, well not to stay anyway. Yvonne wasn't at all pleased when I went round to pick up some of my stuff. That's an understatement; bloody hysterical, more like. And we'd talk a bit, and I'd calm her down a bit. I felt like we were getting to some sort of solution, some sort of compromise."

"Look, you don't have to talk about this if you don't want to, Chris."

"It's alright, Trish. I guess I've started, so, y'know…."

"This sounds ominous."

"Yeah. One evening, a couple of weeks or so later, Yvonne phones me at Phil's. Says she's going to take an overdose if I don't go back. I wasn't impressed after her last attempt and I called her bluff, but this time she wasn't bluffing."

"You'll have to excuse me for a minute…" Melanie suddenly gets up from her chair and rushes from the room, looking even paler than usual. Trisha and I look at one another, wondering what all that's about.

"My story wasn't that bad, was it?"

She returns a couple of minutes later, composed once again.

"Sorry about that. Too much wine I think. Started before you got here. Carry on with your version of events."

A funny way of putting things, I thought, but I carried on as requested.

"So Yvonne didn't turn up at her office the next morning, and the first I heard about what had happened to her was when her friend Sheila phoned me and just screamed obscenities down the phone. Yvonne had washed the tablets down with a lot of whisky, and……….I'm sorry. I should've been there to stop her."

"Would've saved everybody a lot of grief if you'd just gone when she called, obviously."

"Obviously, but like I said, I thought it was a wind-up again."

"So you don't blame yourself for what happened to her?"

"But it wasn't Chris's fault, Mel. I mean it's horrible, but, well obviously he knew her and I didn't, but from what he's told me, she comes across as a bit, er…..deranged."

"That seems a bit harsh, although it's interesting to see your point of view as well. I suppose you would side with Chris…...Deranged…...I would have thought that fragile was a better word. She undoubtedly could've done with some kind of help."

"In hindsight, yes, you're right. Don't want to speak ill of the dead, but that was a terrible thing for her to leave him with though. Not exactly loving. But, yes, sorry. Obviously she needed some kind of help."

"It was a long time ago Mel, way before I moved down here. I've tried to put it behind me. But after all this time there's no way of knowing whether she meant to kill herself or whether it was a stupid accident, like she thought I'd turn up and find her in time. Whatever; I could've stopped her, but there's no use imagining I can turn the clock back, is there?"

"If only we could, Chris. If only we could. And does this ever come into your dreams? You didn't mention anything like this in the stuff you sent me, even though it's clearly had quite some impact on your life. Not enough to haunt you at night though."

"No it doesn't seem to be. Don't know why. She does come into my dreams sometimes, but, weirdly, always in a situation she was never in; she always lives in an old Victorian first floor flat, sometimes with children she never had, sometimes with different partners, but never any suicide."

Melanie leaves the dream topic to ask, "So what did you do after that? After Yvonne died."

"I just flipped for a bit. Took some time owing to get away from work and just disappeared for a couple of weeks to clear my head. It was difficult at work. Yvonne was very popular in her branch and with a few of our colleagues knowing that we were involved, shall we say, it was suggested that some of them were going to find it uncomfortable working with me for a while."

"How did your wife….Carla, was it? How did she react?

"Tactfully enough at first, not to add any more grief, but clearly horrified to be linked in any way to a scandal and phrases like "irresponsible nut-job" didn't take long to come into our heated conversations. And when I took up the offer of a transfer to a position in the south of England I really got some stick, because I wasn't there for Stevie."

"So that's how come you're down here?"

"That's it. Worked down here till they made me redundant in my mid forties, mooched around looking for something to do, found work in the café, met this long-suffering angel, and I think you've been around for most of the rest of it."

Trisha butts in; "Maybe it's about time we were getting going Chris. A lot to do in the morning."

"It's Sunday tomorrow, Trish. Have another drink."

"Love to Mel, but we're meeting up with Steve halfway up the country and we can't afford a hangover."

"Oh yeah…" Oh yeah?

"Fair enough, but before you whizz off, how did things go with Stevie when you moved away? You obviously didn't lose touch completely."

"No, I was still driving up most weekends to see him, but his mother kept making a big thing about me not being "there" for him, almost as if my being a couple of hundred miles down the road when he tripped in the school playground was a crime. Sorry, that sounds a bit callous doesn't it. But any opportunity to make me feel less than supportive emotionally, she'd use it. Stevie was always happy to see me, but the question, "Daddy, why do you have to live so far away?" came up a lot and my answer never sounded convincing enough, not even to me."

"Chris……"

"Yes, okay, we're going. Thanks Mel; great help, all that stuff."

"Was it? I'm not sure we scratched much of the surface. You've left me with something to think about anyway. I did have some other ideas, but maybe I could email them to you for now, and of course you know you're welcome to come back any time."

"Great idea. Now let's get going before Greg comes in and starts crowing over his victory or something and telling me it's a good job I wasn't there to spoil his chances."

We don't manage to dodge that particular bullet though. We hear the front door open and Greg clumsily taking his shoes off. Even with what was probably an ox-felling amount of beer he does his best to follow the house rules.

His big craggy head pokes round the door, his complexion somewhat rosier than when he went out.

"Still here then I see. She hasn't turned you into newts yet?"

"I'm not going to come back with the next line, Greg, just in case there's a copyright issue."

"That was quite funny for you, Chris. Too late for a quick run through of the Parrot Sketch? Never mind. Hey! We rocked tonight. You should've seen me on the maths round. Greg Rainham? I was more like Greg Rain Man."

"Was it his shy smile and modesty that first attracted you, Mel? He's certainly won me over."

"Very droll, Chris. Have I ever told you about when I won my lovely wife over?"

He had, but he's hard to stop.

"Not now, Greg, if you don't mind. They were just about to go."

"It won't take long. Just the basic facts, ma'am," as he takes a gulp from the last bottle of red, adding to the considerable quantity of beverages already consumed. The bottle is replaced on the table with more force than he intended, so he picks it up again. "We were all up in Hebden Bridge, the old uni crowd. Very arty-farty sort of place and a real hot bed of, well, hot beds. Nudge, nudge. Back in those days Mel was into all this dreamy, hippy stuff. Looked bloody good in a kaftan; bloody good. Still does for that matter."

"Greg, you really should go and sleep it off. You're embarrassing me."

"That's because you've switched into 'happily married woman with two squabbling teenagers' mode. But in the old days we never knew if we were going to get beads and flowers or crucifixes and pentagrams. The Divine Ms R we used to call her. She'd read your Tarot cards as soon as look at you."

"Greg, enough! Or it won't be "happily" for much longer!" And amazingly she succeeds in propelling her bulky and resistant husband across the room in the direction of the stairs. He shouts back over his shoulder, gesturing with the not quite empty bottle, "And I managed to cure her of the other thing Hebden Bridge is famous for, and I don't mean going on narrow-boat holidays."

Melanie pushes him up the stairs:

"I'll be down in a minute," she says with an exasperated look.

"Not if I have anything to do with it! See yourselves out."

So we did.

"Do they still live in caves where Greg comes from? I have to say, if I were married to him, a very unlikely scenario ever, I'd be back up to Hebden Bridge like a shot."

"Oo-er, missus. Yes, I do sometimes wonder what she sees in that unreconstructed chauvinist. Heart of gold, of course, though it possibly doesn't compensate for the Neanderthal mind. So what was all that about? Going to meet Steve tomorrow? News to me."

"Just a ruse to get you to stop talking. I've heard you beating yourself up so many times at home, I just didn't want to see you doing it again in public."

"Mel's not exactly public now, is she?"

"Course not. But I expect she's going to be on the phone, milking me for details at every opportunity. Anyway, what did you think about what she came up with? Not exactly full of earth shattering revelations I thought."

"Not exactly, but the bit about being threatened by some aspect of my own personality made me think, although it doesn't take a rocket scientist to tell you that your dreams are based on what's in your own mind. I don't know if she was trying to say that the old man in the dreams is an aspect of me?"

"You're driving like an old man! Could you get a move on so we can get home and get some sleep? I drank a lot of that wine while you were talking and I feel rubbish now."

I look across at Trisha, who has her eyes closed, probably to keep out street lights and approaching car headlights. I speed up a bit, but try to keep our journey home as smooth as possible; don't want her throwing up in the car. Suspending the conversation gives me too much time to think about the way things have worked out over the years and how I feel about it.

I know that Carla and I had married much too young. We'd both admitted that. We got together, madly in love, in our late teens and, for her family, marriage was the only decent option if we were determined to be together. My family were all for it too and we were just swept along in the excitement and euphoria of it all. Seemed like a good idea to me at the time, but in hindsight, celebrating your first wedding anniversary before your twenty-first birthday bash is just wrong. I suppose saying that we were pushed into marrying much too young smacks of self-justification for subsequent bad behaviour, because to be fair, it's not as if I was forcibly marched to the altar. I was every bit as full of enthusiasm for the wedding as everybody else and fully complicit in all the organising, but it was much later that I gradually came to resent the received wisdom that had encouraged us to make such a commitment when we were not much more than kids. If Steve had been planning to get married that young I'd have told him he was mad. Thinking about it, he probably had more sense at that age anyway.

So somewhere along the way I ballsed up in the worst way and Carla and I split up after about twelve years, twelve years that weren't all bad I have to admit. Along with the resentment went a sense of failure, because even though people kept telling me it takes two to make or break a marriage, I felt like it was my fault that it had gone wrong, and I don't like failing at anything or letting people down. Carla was quite happy to let me take the blame and, as I'd told Melanie earlier, drip-fed the idea that I was a pretty lousy father too. Spoon-fed? Shovel-fed?

What with all that and Yvonne's death, I've been beating myself up for years, as Trish said. By contrast, I'm proud to say that I never let anybody down at work. Dead reliable, me; you can always count on Chris. But that's not entirely what life's about, is it? So I do sometimes wonder whether I'm only superficially a good man and I can't help it nagging away at me that somewhere along the line I'll let Trisha down too.

That night I dreamt of my death. Must ask Mel what that means. I was dead, with multiple versions of my corpse, all wrapped in cling film. Definitely don't know what that's all about. It was just a dream this time; I didn't wake up covered in cling film, but at least I woke up.

As promised, later in the week Melanie came through with some more dream interpretations, the idea that bicycles are devices providing assistance for our endeavours; was I riding, pushing, uphill, downhill. Was the road flat? Or it could be a desire for freedom without responsibility. Did I want to be absolved of responsibility for my actions? she asked. Bad enough me beating myself up, without Melanie shaping up to join in. Her attitude in our conversation at her house was quite unlike her usual happy-go-lucky demeanour. She seemed almost judgmental, and her rapid exit to the bathroom looked as if it was caused by more than a full bladder. We never got round to discussing that.

Like I said, her insights into my dreams are not so much a science, more a catalyst for introspection, but then I do plenty of that anyway. Still, every little helps.

Successfully completed journeys indicate a satisfactory completion of our aims, she said. I suppose the guaranteed failure to complete any journeys in my dreams might suggest the opposite then. ("Is that obvious too, Mel?") Being lost on the journey suggests mental or emotional confusion and a loss of ability or motivation to make clear decisions. This all sounds like it's right up my street; introspection and confusion. I'm starting to lean towards my earlier appraisal of all this being mumbo-jumbo though, and that she hasn't told me anything yet that I couldn't have guessed at for myself.

And death could mean change…..isn't that the same with Tarot cards? I'll have to ask her.

Change was just around the corner.

I went to bed and continued to read Mel's email there, but I could see that it wasn't helping Trisha get to sleep. I was wide awake though, so I decided to go downstairs and, just for a change, go out for a walk. It was a beautiful clear night and I like the sight of the full moon. Bit of a loony, I have often quipped. Too often, I'm told. I felt a lot better after the walk, and tired, but I decided to crash out on the sofa instead of going back to bed. I took off my jacket, shoes and socks, checked my phone for messages, stuck it back in my pocket, put on the headphones and I was asleep within minutes.

Here Today, Gone Tomorrow

Trisha wakes up at around eight as usual, anticipating the coffee that Chris would be making in the kitchen, but she can't hear the usual sounds of the grinder. "Wake up and smell the coffee"; the overworked expression enters her head, but strangely, she can't smell any coffee. Pity, she could do with the drink; last night's sleep was a bit disturbed. She'd had that bizarre dream with the pink dog again, chasing it for what seemed like miles and trying to grab its bright green lead. The dog always escaped just as she thought she'd caught it.

She puts on her dressing gown and goes downstairs:

"Chris! Chris?"

The amp and CD player are still on, his socks are on the floor in front of the sofa and his shoes are by the door, but he's not in the kitchen and the kettle is stone cold. This is very confusing, but he might have gone out into the garden. The back door's locked though and, when she checks, so is the front door, with the chain on. All the keys are still hanging up.

"Come on Chris. This isn't funny. You're too old to be playing hide 'n' seek."

That should get him out; he's very sensitive about his age. The internal access door to the garage is still locked, with the key on the inside. He must be in one of the other bedrooms upstairs, although she can't think why. No, not in any of the bedrooms, so she starts to look in unlikely places, like their bed, just in case he'd come back to bed during the night and she'd got up without noticing him there.

She goes back downstairs to have a rethink. His phone! She can't see it, but if she calls it she might hear it ringing, and if he's gone out he's probably got his phone on him. But how can he have gone out with everything locked.......?

She presses the button to call his phone. It doesn't ring in the house or get through to Chris. Instead she hears "The number you have dialled has not been recognised." What?!

Through the living room window she notices a movement outside, but it's not Chris. It's their next door neighbour, returning from the shops with his paper. Trisha unlocks the front door and calls, "Mike, you haven't seen Chris on your travels have you?"

"No love. Has he gone AWOL?"

"Er, no, it's alright. He's probably nipped out for some milk." But he hasn't taken the car, she notices, but how could he? The keys are still there, and his shoes and socks.

For the first time Trisha starts to think that her practical nature isn't enough to cope with this. She has run out of reasonable ideas and is wracking her brains to think of anything that might give her a clue to his whereabouts. What day is it? Sunday. She phones the landline at their shop. There shouldn't be anybody there on a Sunday morning, but maybe Chris popped round for something. She tries to remember if he'd had any new trainers delivered, to account for why his usual ones were still in the house.

For no particularly logical reason she calls Melanie, although needing a friend to talk to is quite a logical reason under the circumstances she thinks. And she was one of the last people they'd seen recently.

"Mel! I can't find Chris….."

"What do you mean, you can't find Chris?"

"Just that. I got up this morning and he's not here. But the house is completely locked from the inside. It doesn't make sense." Trisha hears Mel relaying this to Greg, and Greg's muffled reply.

"Greg says to check the loft; he's probably up there cataloguing his cassette collection. Look, Greg, Trisha's really upset about this."

Trisha, realising how true this is, finds her eyes filling up with tears and her voice catches as she tells Melanie she's going to have another look round.

"Trish, you don't think he's just gone shopping without you, do you?"

"Of course not, and the car's still here."

"Look, I'm coming over. This is intriguing. Give me twenty minutes."

While she's waiting Trisha thinks that maybe it would be a good idea to let Steve know what was going on, not that she knew what the hell was going on herself. It was just possible, of course, that Chris had been in touch with his son. Anything seemed possible at this point.

"Hello Trisha. How're ya doing?" Steve and Trisha had always got on really well on the few occasions each year that they met up.

"Steve! Sorry to pester you on a Sunday morning, but I'm really worried about your dad. No, he's not ill as far as I know. I just can't find him." She runs through the history of her fruitless search so far, parrying all of his suggestions with her insistence that she has looked everywhere.

"You don't think he's up to his old tricks do you? Hate to ask…." His mother's influence is still there, Trisha notices.

"No I don't. And even if he were, he'd have to be Houdini to get out of here. That's the thing I can't understand."

"Well I would give it a bit longer, but maybe phoning the police might be a good idea if he doesn't show up soon. Or do you want me to call them?"

Trisha suddenly feels very shaky at the thought that this might have escalated to the point of being a police matter. Surely there must be a simple explanation to all this. There always is, isn't there?

"No, I'll do it if I have to. Good idea though. Just keep in touch. I've got a friend coming over and I think I can hear her car now, so got to go."

"Right you are. I'll be there if you need me."

Trisha and Melanie meet with a hug at the front door. Mel can see her friend has been crying and suggests going to the kitchen so that she can make them both tea while they talk through what's happening. Trish becomes even more upset when she thinks that only an hour or so ago she was looking forward to the morning coffee ritual with her husband.

"Chris didn't seem particularly upset when you were round at ours. I know he's a bit taken up with his dreams at the moment, but I didn't think that telling me about his past was a huge problem for him. It didn't sound like a guilty conscience was going to ruin his life. Was he alright after you left?"

"I think so. He seemed a bit thoughtful, but he's behaved perfectly normally ever since. He was sitting up in bed last night reading your emails again, but I don't think there was anything in them to make him suddenly decide to run away, do you?"

"No. Even I have to admit it was all a bit vague. Look, you finish your tea while I have a look round. Fresh pair of eyes 'n' all that. I'll look under the bed."

Trisha gives Melanie five minutes before she decides to join her. She can hear her moving around in the bedroom and thinks that, of all places, she won't find him under the bed. She walks into the room as Mel straightens up from, sure enough, looking under the bed.

"Well either you two are into some really kinky stuff or you've got a dog that I didn't know about."

In her hand is a bright green dog lead.

"Trisha! What's wrong? You look like you've seen a ghost."

The Force Is With Her

The non-emergency police number, 101, seemed like the best place to start, and if the calm and businesslike person on the other end of the phone thought that calling only two hours after her husband had gone walkabout was a bit soon, she didn't labour the point. Husbands go straying all the time, her own being a case in point, but she tried to keep the cynicism at bay because the caller seemed very distressed as she described what sounded like an Agatha Christie locked room mystery, and so she assured her that, no, you don't have to wait twenty four hours to report a missing person and that she would arrange for a couple of officers to visit as soon as possible, hopefully by the end of the morning.

Putting the phone down, Trisha thought that Mel appeared to be as baffled by the discovery of the dog lead as she was herself. Well baffled was better than terrified, which was her first reaction when she saw it. She'd been sceptical when Chris told her he'd been seeing things from his dreams, but now it had happened to her. What the fuck? Surely this didn't happen to everybody. She had a sudden thought of it being a topic for the Jeremy Kyle show: "My Husband Finds All These Things In His Dreams, He Says!", or a premium paid on Ebay for genuine ex-dream artefacts. No, this wasn't a widespread phenomenon, so why was it happening to them?

But Chris's words came back to her: "I can't go to the police and tell them I'm being stalked by an old man from my dreams, and he's carrying some curtains," or words to that effect. "They'll put me in a padded cell."

She now found herself in the same situation. It's one thing reporting a missing husband, quite another to say that you've come into possession of a dog lead that was in your dream last night. But Chris....where is he?

If there's truth in the adage "policemen are getting younger all the time", often used by those reaching middle-age and beyond, then the pair that turned up on Trisha's doorstep in the middle of the day were the epitome of the expression. Trisha thought it couldn't have been all that long since they were trying on policemen's helmets from the dressing up box at pre-school. She didn't say that. But there was no faulting their professional and sympathetic handling of her plight. Obviously they thought, and who can blame them, that the missing husband would walk through the door very soon and apologise for wasting police time, and they would "not at all, Sir", and leave him and his wife to deal with the fallout from whatever dodgy excuse he'd managed to invent.

But they didn't say that. They asked Trisha when she had last seen her husband and why she thought he was missing. So she took them round the house and explained how all the doors were still locked when she got up and all the keys were still hanging up, and pointed to the clothes that he'd left behind on the living room floor.

"Is it possible, Mrs Adwell, that your husband could have a key that you don't know about?"

"Of course it's possible; he could have cut one himself. It's one of the things we do in our shop. And we have enough spare keys already. But even if he had one, he couldn't have put the chain back on the door from the outside could he?"

"No, I suppose not. But we had to ask." And they continued to ask: did she know of any reason why he might have gone out, had she contacted anybody who might know where he was, had he been acting strangely or differently recently?

"Not at all. I'd say our lives are consistently, pleasantly er...boring, just the way we both like it." She says that, but she's thinking about dreams and padded cells; don't go there. "But it still doesn't explain how he got out of a locked house, does it?"

Looking out of their depth with that one, the two officers decide to examine the doors and locks again. One of them goes off to do that, escorted by Melanie, who has stayed for moral support, while the other takes down more details about the missing Chris: has he taken anything with him, or left anything behind that he might usually take if he went out? Does he have a health condition that we should be concerned about? Could we have details of friends and relatives that he might visit, or places he regularly goes to? Did she know what he was wearing and could she supply a recent photograph?

The lock inspector returns with a baffled shake of his head, and the pair make a move to leave.

"So what happens now?"

"Okay, well this is your reference number. Call the number you contacted us on, the 101, with this reference if you hear anything from your husband. All the details you've given us will be circulated to all UK police forces within forty-eight hours, but obviously, if he doesn't come back then keep in touch and we'll have the inquiry stepped up. But most people do turn up very soon in our experience, so please don't worry Mrs Adwell."

She closed the front door behind them and Trisha was left feeling that the officers had done all that could reasonably be expected of them, but that somebody like Hercule Poirot would have done something more. Where's a fictional detective with brilliant little grey cells when you need one?

Living The Dream 2

I open my eyes and notice that it's already light outside, but the light is filtered through the curtains and there's not enough to define the details in the room. There's no rush; I had a good night's sleep on the sofa and I'm sure there's plenty of time to ease myself into the day before I put the kettle on. I can hear the garden birds getting their day organised. One particularly vocal blackbird is doing that thing they do, berating some poor bloody cat, most likely ours, for the sheer cheek of existing in feline form.

Maybe some more music then. I stretch out my right hand to feel around for my headphones, which must have fallen somewhere during the night, but I strike it against some unexpected hard object. It feels like the corner of a table. And then I realise that I'm not lying on the sofa. I'm sprawled in an armchair. We haven't got an armchair, just two big sofas. Is this another dream? Wouldn't surprise me. And here's me thinking that I'd got away with it. So where am I this time?

Then I hear the sound of somebody descending a staircase and I tense myself as whoever it is approaches. The door into the room opens and even in the half-light I realise it's another "Back with Carla" dream; not my worst nightmare, but bad enough. Funny; I thought I was awake, but obviously I'm not. She speaks and something of a dim memory stirs in my mind.

"You're still here then. I thought I heard you drive away in the middle of the night"

Carla reaches for the wall switch and while I'm blinking in the sudden flood of light, she lets out a deafening scream. Jesus, what the hell was that for? That's the kind of pivotal event in a dream that would normally have me waking up thinking "Jesus, what the hell was that all about?" but, no, I'm still here with Carla, who is now pointing at me with a very unsteady hand. But something in my brain reasons that this isn't quite right. I don't usually think it's just another "Back with Carla" dream while I'm actually dreaming it. I'm just, well I'm just there, feeling defeated and disappointed.

"What on earth has happened to your face?"

I don't know. What on earth has happened to my face? I instinctively put my hands to my face and it all seems pretty normal to me.

"What do you mean?" thinking I've got some food on it or something.

"Just go and look in the mirror!"

So I do, and I think, "Yes, that's me alright. Nothing stuck on my face. Could probably do with a shave though."

"And what the hell are you wearing?" And I look down at my bare feet and grey Levis and a tee shirt printed with Roger Waters' In The Flesh Tour 2002.

"Has that bitch got you on some kind of recreational drugs or something, because I can't think of any other explanation for what's happened to you?"

I turn back to the mirror and an icy tingle starts to run through the hair on my scalp and my heart starts pounding. I feel faint and unsteady; this is so realistic it almost feels like I'm not dreaming, that I've woken up….but that's impossible. Isn't it?

Carla is standing there, looking distressed, waiting for some kind of response from me I suppose. It's all too realistic, too detailed. If this were a dream I would expect to be jumping on a bike and pedalling up the stairs at any moment, or seeing Carla turn into some wizened old git who brusquely orders me out of the house.

"I'm sorry. I don't understand what's happening," is all I can think to say. I'm waiting for that point in the dream where the stress wakes me up. I'll get my bearings and breathe a sigh of relief. While I'm waiting there's a knock at the door. Carla breaks off from our staring match to go and answer it. I hear a muffled conversation and then she returns with a single letter.

"It's for you. I don't know why he had to knock, but it wasn't our usual postman. A really old man; looked like he should be retired by now."

I rushed past her before she could finish what she was saying and yanked the front door open, but there was nobody there, nobody in the street at all. How could an old man have disappeared out of the street two hundred yards long in a matter of seconds, unless I'm still dreaming? But the letter in my hand looks and feels real enough though. It's addressed to me and I can just make out the postmark: Oxford, March something, 2018.

If it's addressed to me I'd better open it. There's a single sheet of paper inside and, handwritten, the message reads:

**No, you're not dreaming.
And your wife misses you**.

What do people say? I had to pinch myself to see if I was dreaming. Well, I pinched myself, pulled my hair, slapped my face a couple of times before I came to the conclusion that I've been trying to avoid; I'm not dreaming. This is a nightmare. Well obviously it isn't, because I'm not dreaming. A nightmare come true? I hardly have time to adjust to any of this before Carla is standing at the living room door, demanding that I come back in and explain what the hell is going on. So I follow her back in, but I don't fancy her chances of getting an explanation.

"What's in the letter?" I don't particularly want her to read it, especially the bit about my wife.

"Nothing important." I try to sound casual, but not very convincingly, and she snatches it out of my hand.

"No, you're right. Just an invoice for car tyres." What!? "Were you expecting something else? Why the big rush to see the postman?" There's a pattern developing here; I have no answers for her and it's clear that my lack of any reasonable explanation is beginning to annoy her. I'm not feeling any too rosy about it either. She returns to the theme of my appearance, but before I have the opportunity to explain why I look like I've aged considerably overnight, the door opens again and in stumbles Stevie, rubbing his eyes and probably wondering why his mother screamed a few minutes earlier. He sees me and joins in the critique of my appearance; "Daddy, what's happened to your hair?" He doesn't look especially alarmed. Carla and I are both way ahead of him in that regard. I'm shaking now and I have to sit down on something. I've lived through this day before, but not quite like this. In fact not at all like this. But if Carla is talking about The Bitch it must be after she discovered my affair with Yvonne. The day after? "You're still here then," she said.

Yes, apparently I'm literally back there, in the flesh. Not a dream. I'm convinced now that this is all making too much sense to be a dream. No; not making sense; too linear. None of it makes sense. And the realisation is terrifying me.

Again I tell myself that it can't be happening, but then all the other stuff that I believed was happening, all the stuff that was appearing out of my dreams; that couldn't be happening either. Could it?

"Chris, what's happened?" She's a little more concerned now. I guess twelve years or so of love and care don't evaporate overnight. Perhaps I'm just flattering myself to think that she might care after what she'd discovered about me. And I wish I had an understandable answer for her, but I can at least understand the scream. When she went to bed last night I was a healthy, if unhappy, thirty-one year old and now I'm standing, no, sitting before her as a fifty-eight year old. I don't care how well you look after yourself, there's going to be a noticeable difference. I know what Stevie means; the hair's a lot greyer and more sparsely distributed.

"Carla, I don't know what's happened, but it's not drugs. You know I wouldn't do drugs."

"I thought I knew you wouldn't do drugs. There's a lot of things I thought you wouldn't do. But can you find any other explanation? Are you ill?"

Right now, yes, I feel very ill; sick with fear and I'm only just starting to work through the implications of what's going on. I'm certainly not convinced that saying that I've just come back from the spring of 2018 to see how you were getting on would do anything to calm the situation. It's not doing anything to calm me!

Implications! Trisha! What the hell will she be doing right now? I mean if I'm here…….how do I get back to…….can I get back? I'm beyond feeling unsteady on my feet now; I can hardly cope with sitting on a chair.

Carla has gone to the front window and she opens the curtains.

"The car's not there. I was right. You did go out last night. I heard you drive off at about three. So how did you get back? And where's the car?"

I lift my head out of my hands. No, I definitely didn't use the car. But trying to explain my mode of transport was going to be difficult, especially as I didn't know myself. Another thought occurs to me. In fact the thoughts are queuing up waiting to be interviewed, but the first one is "where is my 1991 self right now?". I'm trying to remember what happened after Carla and I rowed the night before; last night, I suppose you could say. I'm certain I stayed here, at least for part of the night. I am absolutely sure that I didn't go to the hospital to find out what had happened to Yvonne, otherwise I'd have discovered her subterfuge with the pills much earlier. God, how differently things might have turned out. So where did I go? If I think hard enough I'll remember what I did, but there's something not quite right here. As far as I remember, I fell asleep in the armchair. I didn't go out in the car to see Yvonne.

So if Chris Adwell Version '91.0 went out last night, where did he go? And what happens if he comes back? Aren't there some kind of rules in time-travel fiction about the inadvisability of meeting your past or future self? The probably unanswerable questions are practically falling over each other to be heard. Is this time-travel and is it fiction?

Carla, presumably realising she's not going to hear anything that she might consider sensible out of me, has disappeared into the kitchen. I can hear the kettle warming up and cups chinking together. I remember that it will be instant granule stuff and not fresh beans, but I'm in no position to argue, that's assuming she's making me one too. Stevie is watching me a little apprehensively from the other side of the room, not used to seeing his father shaking like a leaf in an autumn wind. I'm suddenly overwhelmed with the memory of all the crap that Stevie has in store for him over the next few years, and that I'm largely the cause of it. Does it really take two to ruin a marriage? That's what they say, but they aren't here trying to deal with this, are they?

My negative self analysis is interrupted by the cat walking in, presumably having had enough of the ear-bashing from the blackbird. She immediately starts rubbing her face against my legs.

"Tiggy! Good to see you again." It's nice to see somebody that doesn't look at me with either hostility or apprehension.

I accept the coffee from Carla gratefully, although I don't know why she's put milk in it when she knows I like it black. Maybe it's because she knows I like it black. And then I remember that I started drinking it black because Yvonne did. Was my wife, or rather my ex wife, really that intuitive?

"Well? Care to tell me what's going on yet? Why do you look like you've aged almost twenty years overnight?"

I suppose I should be flattered at that. Should I tell her it's actually nearer thirty? Not yet, I think.

"Look, Carla, I'm not entirely sure myself, but I've got half an idea and I know you're going to think it's ridiculous."

"Anything would help, ridiculous or not. This is really scaring me."

"What's the date today?"

"What's that got to do with it?"

"Please!"

"April 17th"

"And what year?"

"Oh come on! 1991 of course!"

How do I put this? "When I went to sleep last night it was March 2018."

I hadn't really had much hope in that being a winning line and I was right. She just stared at me for about ten seconds, confusion competing with hostility.

"That's ridiculous." Told you. "And pathetic. Who do you think you are? Doctor Who?"

Good one. At least Doctor Who always had an assistant; I feel very alone right now. I could do with a little help, somebody to explain to me how I can explain the impossible to a person that no longer trusts me anyway. Some sort of phrasebook for use in uncharted territory would be useful.

"I think you need to see a doctor as soon as possible. There must be some physical reason for why you've gone like this overnight. I'm going to phone the surgery as soon as they open and see if you can get an appointment today."

"Okay, well that seems like a good idea. Thank you." I'm not going to argue; while Carla is being practical she's not completely freaking out and it gives me time to think, something I very much need. At the mention of the word "phone" I suddenly remember that I still have my phone in my pocket. I'm surprised that I haven't reached for it already. In 2018 we don't just turn to our phones in times of crisis; we do it all the time, checking Facebook, emails, Instagram, text messages, football scores, the weather, Facebook again in case we missed something the first time we looked. It's obsessive behaviour.

I could try to get in touch with Trisha, but then I realise that 1991 won't have very good network coverage, will it? The sense of despair and isolation descends on me again, but Carla interrupts this because she has noticed my move towards my pocket.

"What's that in your pocket?" Telling her to mind her own business probably wouldn't go down very well either, or the gag about being pleased to see her.

Reluctantly I pull out my i-Phone 5. I know it's probably due an upgrade already, but nobody in 1991 has seen anything like this.

"What on earth have you been wasting our money on now? What is that thing?"

The most plausible sounding description I can come up with is that it's a sort of combined calculator and camera and that I was issued with it at work.

"The film cartridge must be tiny to fit in there. Is it like microfilm or something?"

"Something like that. It stores the pictures on a memory card inside." Oops, I've said too much.

"Wow Dad! Can I see? Have you got pictures in it?"

And so I make the mistake of getting up and going over to show Stevie how to access the photographs and scroll through them. He could do with some attention and I could do with a distraction, and besides, I haven't seen him for twenty seven years either. Hey! A positive at last. The only positive thing so far though. Most fathers just have photographs of what their kids looked like when they were small. I'm getting a live reminder. Nice to have a little father and son moment in all of this stress. But of course the phone has lots of pictures of Trisha.

"Who's this lady, Daddy?" Damn!

"You're not showing him pictures of that...that...?"

I don't think Trisha would appreciate being referred to as "that bitch" but I remember that Carla had never actually met Yvonne. She'd only just become aware of her existence the previous evening.

Carla comes over to look at the phone.

"Is that her? Get that thing away from Stevie!" And she swipes and knocks the phone out of my hands. Good job it's in a case.

"No, that's not her…." Why do I keep blundering into these conversational disaster areas?

"Do you mean you've got another one on the go?"

"No! Look, I told you…Oh, forget it. Yes, make a doctor's appointment and I'll see if he can find a name for whatever this is," knowing that he won't, but I need a break while I figure out what's behind all this, or who, or how. I realise I'm starting to get quite angry; frustrated I guess. Carla becomes defensive.

"Don't start shouting at me. I've had a lot to put up with from you in the last twenty four hours, and now you come in here looking like an old man!"

Gee, thanks.

"I'm sorry, really. It's not your fault. Look, if I'm going to have to go to the doctor's could I have some of my clothes? I can't go like this."

"I'll get you some. You're not going back in my bedroom again, even to get clothes. So how come you're wearing a tee shirt for a concert that hasn't happened yet?"

"I did try to tell you, but you said it was ridiculous."

I study her face, looking for a glimmer of understanding, something to indicate that she accepts at least a part of what I've said, but no. With a derisory shake of her head she goes upstairs to find me some clothes. I am permitted to change in the bathroom.

"Is it still through the kitchen?"

"What do you mean? It was last night! Honestly!"

I'm glad to see that my clothes still fit me pretty well after twenty seven years, as long as I pull my stomach in quite a bit. Sorry, Dr Peterson; needs must. While I'm getting dressed I have time to think about something that occurred to me while we were looking at my phone's pictures. Yvonne's name came up and I suddenly realised that I have arrived at a point in time several months before her death. That means I could save her, prevent her from killing herself. Could I save her? I don't know. All she'd wanted was for me to answer her call for help and I ignored her. Now I have a chance to put things right.

Wait a minute; if I do that, assuming it's even possible, would that change everything else that happened to me? Would I ever meet Trisha? Trisha! What must she be thinking right now? Unless, of course I've already somehow changed the future and she doesn't even know who I am. This can't be happening; I used to really like my future, but now I don't think it'll be what it once was.

If I really have been somehow picked up and deposited in my own past, what are the implications of my being here? Is it a good or bad thing? I know what's in store for Stevie. Perhaps I could spare him all that trouble, all that being caught between parents who don't see eye to eye on anything any more. Or I could have been around more to be a better, supportive father. Then I never would have known Trisha!

I can't help wondering why it has to be this particular date in my past, and once again I fall back on the thought that perhaps it is some super detailed dream. But no; I've already established that it isn't. If not, then am I being used by somebody? Manipulated? Because this couldn't just happen by chance, surely. I haven't heard of it happening to anybody else, although maybe that's because they never came back. Oh shit! People do disappear without any explanation, don't they, or without ever being found again. Is that what I'll become, eventually just a statistic, the file closed, missing presumed dead? Almost as bad is the thought that, let's see, I'm fifty-eight now; if I stay stuck here in this time zone, for want of a better expression, I'll be eighty-bloody-five in 2018. If I turn up at Trisha's then, assuming I can find her, she'll think…….God knows what she'll think, but I'll be older than her father.

Once again I'm shaking with fear and I sit down on the side of the bath. If this were fiction I would probably muster up some sort of heroic qualities and look for a way out of my predicament. So far I've spent most of my time sitting down, a quivering wreck. I have to do something. I start by picking myself up and going back to find Carla, who is getting on with the business of the day, like putting Stevie's breakfast on the dining room table. Now that all the curtains are open I get a clearer view of the room, and on a shelf in an alcove to one side of the chimney breast stands a pair of ornaments; a porcelain boy and girl at a picnic, a blue tit on a branch and to the right of them, a blue-white ceramic pot of yellow roses.

Dog Tired

Trisha is living the worst day of her life. It has been five hours since the two policemen left with the vaguely encouraging observation that most people turn up within a few hours. But this is not the sort of thing her Chris does, even for a few hours. If this is some kind of joke, well he knows she'd never find it even remotely funny.

Although she told the police that her life with Chris was unremarkable, even boring, and they liked it that way, it wasn't really like that. Life was comfortable and warm and they were happy with their home and business and country walks, at least she'd always thought that they were. There was nothing she could see to indicate that Chris was unhappy or wanted to leave. She didn't think he'd just walked out, and as she'd kept insisting, how could he, from a locked house?

Which brought her to the disturbing existence of the dog lead that Melanie had found in the bedroom. For the first time she started to seriously consider what Chris had been saying to her about his dreams. Seriously considering and understanding were still miles apart though. Melanie appeared as unsettled by the presence of the lead as Trisha was. Nothing in her theoretical dream interpretation covered objects following you out of your dreams. She did agree with Trisha, that keeping this discovery from the police might be a good idea for the moment.

Reluctantly, Melanie had had to go home, promising that she would return later to see how Trisha was getting on. Left on her own, Trisha wasn't getting on very well. She and Chris never spent very much time apart. She missed him even if he was gone for a few hours, even if she knew exactly where he was and what time he would be back. If he was running late without letting her know she got really stressed. She knew that some people might think that was an unhealthy relationship, but it worked for them. Some people can think what they like.

But this was torture. She didn't make herself feel any better by Googling police procedures for tracing a missing person. She read that they might want to have a DNA sample, perhaps by bagging and taking away his toothbrush. A horrible vision of Chris's body being found and having to be identified from DNA came and tormented her. Then she read that if the police located him alive they were under no obligation to tell her where he was if he didn't want them to.

The day dragged on. She phoned her mother, and then her sister. Repeating the story to them just led to the same unhelpful, though understandable reactions: he must have another key, he'll probably turn up later; people do, don't they? was he seeing somebody else? (Thanks, Sis!), could he have early onset dementia? (Bit rich, Mum).

She spoke to Steve again, who was preparing to drive down the next day after he'd dropped his two kids off at school. That's if his dad didn't turn up in the meantime, which of course people do, don't they? Her two recent acquaintances from the local police force also promised to call round again in the morning, unless Chris's return made that unnecessary.

Trisha thanked them and then, as she still had the phone in her hand, decided to call Melanie, to put her off until tomorrow too.

"That's alright Trish, if you're sure you're going to be alright. I'll be there as soon as I can tomorrow. Oh, and by the way, I looked up what dogs mean in dreams after you told me about the pink dog. Dogs represent friends, not necessarily man's best friend, but whether they're good friends or false friends depends on whether the dog is friendly or aggressive. And the colour pink suggests a good outcome, so maybe this will all turn out alright. Chin up!"

Trisha couldn't remember what mood the dog was in, just that it had been running loose, a stray. She realised she was exhausted from all the stress and repeated conversations, and just needed to close her eyes for a while, although whether she could sleep with so much going on in her head she very much doubted.

It could be a long and difficult night, but she thought that the proverbial forty winks on the sofa might be a good idea. She drifted into sleep within minutes.

Memories Are Made Of This

"Where did you get those flowers? The yellow roses," I asked Carla. It came out like an accusation, I realised.

Carla continued to look at me as if she thought I was mad or possessed or something.

"What a ridiculous question! You bought me them last week. I guess that was some kind of guilty conscience thing, given what you've been up to. Don't you remember? Have you got amnesia now as well as grey hair?"

Well obviously I wasn't here last week, not in my twenty-first century incarnation. Perhaps I had bought them; it's the sort of detail that's easy to forget years down the line. I'm dredging the depths of my memory, trying to remember a small detail from 1991. Where did I acquire the bloody plant from? Carla's probably right though; a guilty conscience gift only one step up from petrol station flowers, and it comes back to me now. It came from a local department store that had a garden and housewares section in their basement. Such an effort to remember and yet this reminder of my old home kept invading my dreams so effortlessly. I decided to play along with the amnesia idea to see if she can tell me any more about this bloody plant pot that has become the bane of my life.

"No, I'm sorry. It's all been a bit stressful. I just can't remember when I got them."

"It was last week, on market day. You said you bought them from an old man with a flower stall......Oh what now, for God's sake?"

This collapsing onto the nearest available chair was becoming a habit. If I was going to start being heroic I was going to have a lot of work to do, but perhaps heroes also feel like their insides have turned to water and they shake with fear when they put two and two together and come up with, well not exactly four just yet, but they realise that they're, in all probability, in the shit. As unreliable as a witness is likely to be after almost three decades, I definitely would not have said anything about an old man on the market. So what has happened to the truth? Is somebody putting words in Carla's mouth?

"What day's market day?"

"Oh, for Christ's sake! How long have you lived here?"

About an hour and a half is the correct answer, but she'll see that as facetious I'm sure.

"It's tomorrow, am I right?"

"You know it is; has been for years. But what's that got to do with anything? It's a doctor you need, not a trip to the bloody market."

"No, you're right. I just don't remember buying them at all. Perhaps it is time to try for a doctor's appointment." I have no intention of going to see a doctor, but I need to go along with the idea for now, just to buy me time to think what to do next. I would very much like to meet this old man. Ha! I run the ad in my head: "WLTM old man with a view to discussing shared interests for our mutual benefit". I'm not so sure I can think of any benefit I would like to bring to his life, but I sure would like him to help sort mine out, because I'm certain this whole scene I'm in is being manipulated by somebody. It's not quite the past that I remember. Neither young Chris nor I bought that bloody miniature rose bush from the market last week.

So now I just need to play along with Carla's doctor suggestion, keep her sweet and bide my time until I can find some way to escape to the market tomorrow. I'm assuming a lot here, that the old man will be there at the market, but unless he makes himself accessible before then, it's all I have to go on. I have to say, for a pensioner, he very laudably keeps himself active; dropping off his dry cleaning, running a model shop, making coffee, selling plants on the market. Oh yes. Nearly forgot being a railway guard and officiating at a Nazi death camp. Nice. I hope I can follow his example and stay active after I retire. I'd still like to wring his neck though.

"Look Carla, I'm really sorry about all the shit I've caused you…."

"Too late for that! You needn't bother grovelling your way back, 'cos it won't work."

"I know. I'm not, but I do feel really ill and I need to find out what's happening to me. I feel very confused; can't even remember what I did with the car last night." Which was a lie. I had figured out exactly where the car was. In the early hours of the morning, my younger self had driven off to a meeting at the head office in Wigan and when that was finished, had gone straight back to Yvonne's flat. I'm disappointed by "his" lack of practical concern for Yvonne. Well, my lack of practical concern, to be fair. Christ, I didn't even bother to phone the hospital during the day. What kind of person was I back then? But at least this meant "I" wasn't going to walk in here any time soon and cause who knows what to happen. At the very least, it would be another very stressful experience for Carla. She was having enough trouble coping with the ageing husband in the room now, never mind the contemporary version coming to the party too. I'd predict a massive meltdown, for all of us.

"Fine! Well I've got to take Stevie to pre-school. You call the surgery while I'm out and see if they can fit you in. And, like I said last night, you might as well start packing your stuff, because I want you out of here as soon as possible."

I remember now. She did say that "last night", but I could do with finding a way to stall my ejection until tomorrow, so I can get to the market and see if my tormentor is there. Carla and Stevie head towards the front door and Carla calls back, with a touch of sarcasm in her voice,

"You've probably forgotten the doctor's number too. It's on the list next to the phone."

Glad she told me that. So I ring the surgery and they tell me that they have a slot available in the afternoon, but I tell them that tomorrow morning would be better, so they book me in for then. Carla will be pleased!

I suppose I'd better at least look like I'm packing to leave, but then she'll insist that I do actually leave, and I'd rather stay here. I figure that the less of humanity that comes into contact with a man from the future the better. Actually, to be honest, I'm not really thinking about the rest of humanity. I'm sure the planet would cope with whatever choice of reality was presented to it. I'm just thinking of myself and my greatest need, which is to get back to Trisha in as undisturbed a 2018 as possible.

At this point I have a go at reviewing my to do list:

1. Go to the town market tomorrow and find the old man who sold the plant to "me".
2. Work out a way to save Yvonne from killing herself.
3. Find a way to make young Stevie's future more palatable.
4. Go home.

I'm not sure that any or all of these things are mutually inclusive. Good grief; no wonder I've spent so much of the morning collapsing onto the furniture.

My best plan, I reckon, is to feign as much of an unwell demeanour as I can. Shouldn't be too hard. I've got sick with fear, white as a sheet and shaking like a leaf in my repertoire already. Meanwhile, I'll have a look round. After all, very few of us get the opportunity to go back and visit our former lives and look at the stuff we used to own. Only me?

I look at the CD collection. Good grief; there's the very first album I bought on compact disc: James Taylor's Sweet Baby James. I could do with a friend right now, James. I realise that quite a large quantity of this record collection I actually still have at home, my future home, having done as Carla demanded and packed up my valuables. The anxiety comes back, wondering if I'll ever see home again. What have I done to deserve this?

My attention is taken by the discarded copy of yesterday's newspaper. I pick it up to remind myself of what was going on in the world back in 1991. I remember this. The Gulf War, I read, was just coming to an end and peace was being negotiated. Peace, Ha! Look out world; you ain't seen nothing yet. Wait ten years till 9/11, and the consequent wars in Iraq and Afghanistan.

My eye strays down the page to a completely unrelated story that I don't remember making any impact on me before. The police are asking the public for help in tracing a missing Durham University student who hasn't been seen for three days. Twenty year old Patricia Hallam was last seen leaving…..

I add 'legs turning to jelly' to my list of ailments. Patricia Hallam was Trisha's maiden name.

And that's when I knew for certain that somebody is playing with me, that this is not my real past. I'm pretty sure that if Trish had gone missing at any point in her life it would have come up in conversation. I read the article in the paper: fake news, I'm sure of it.

5. Find Patricia Hallam?

…And Don't Forget To Feed The Cat

The evening after Chris's disappearance, Trisha had managed to get to sleep quite quickly. She was mentally exhausted, but she kept waking up during the night, in tears. Each time she'd check her phone in case he'd called, but there was nothing. She felt so completely and utterly helpless and powerless. In the middle of the night she managed to drag herself from the sofa to the bed. The thought that she'd rarely had to go to bed by herself for the last ten years or so did nothing to relieve the anxiety.

In the morning, when she finally woke up to face the day, she still felt completely helpless, but this was chiefly because she was bound and gagged and tied to a chair in a dingy little room she'd never seen before.

Later that morning Melanie arrived, as promised, and let herself in with the spare key that she kept for when Trisha and Chris went on holiday and needed her to feed the cat. She supposed it would be quite a charitable idea to feed it this morning, having received the information that neither of its owners were there.

She picked up the landline telephone and dialled the non-emergency police number and introduced herself to the operator as Mrs Trisha Adwell, quoting the reference number which she read from the photo library in her mobile.

"We're so sorry to have put you to so much trouble, but my husband has turned up safe and well. At least, he's well now. He'd had a bit of a medical issue and I eventually found him at A & E. But our doctor has suggested a break, so we're going away to our caravan by the coast for a couple of days, and we'll be happy to answer any questions as soon as we get back."

And then she thought she'd better phone Steve to let him know that Trisha was busy picking his dad up from the hospital and had asked her to call him on her behalf, and no, there was no cause for concern.

That done, she left the house to attend to a couple more necessary chores, her plan being to go back and sort the cat out later. The very least she could do really.

You Can't Have Both

As I'd anticipated, Carla was none too thrilled to find that the doctor was unable to see me until the following morning, but she conceded that it would at least give me the opportunity to pack my belongings. I'd by this time given up on worrying about what Chris Minor would think when he came back and discovered I'd packed for him. I didn't think this version of reality was anything but a construct for my benefit, if benefit was the right word in this situation.

Carla relented to the extent of allowing me into our bedroom to remove my clothes from the wardrobe. I thought it would be very interesting to see what the well-dressed man of the Spring of 1991 was wearing, or at least remind myself of what I was wearing. You know that thing we do when we see old pictures of ourselves? OMG! What did I look like?

It turns out that I looked very much the same as I do now. That's the 2018 now, not the inconvenient past that I'm presently in. I don't know whether to feel smug about my ability to forecast fashion trends or to make a note to book myself in for a makeover. If I ever get back.

If I ever get back! The recurring despair that turns my insides to water is never far away and the educational value of this trip down memory lane is insufficient compensation. And I remind myself that the only clue that I've got so far in the sense of a direction to go in is the piece of information that I bought a plant from an old man on the market last week. I'm sure that this piece of information is a plant too, but if I'm wrong then I'll just be going for a walk round the market. Perhaps I should ask Carla if she would like any fruit and veg, just so it's not a completely wasted journey.

This day is going to drag. I pull my phone out again to check the time before remembering that it's probably in a very different time zone. The phone survived its earlier plunge to the floor and the battery is down to about sixty percent. No service, I notice. It hasn't been invented yet. I look at the bedside clock-radio. It's not even midday yet. Really dragging, but in spite of feeling extremely out of sorts, I find myself also feeling very hungry. Huh! Twenty seven years must be the longest gap between meals ever.

I wonder what sort of a day Carla is having. She would have woken up dealing with the misery of our collapsed marriage, probably expecting to impart the news to a good friend or to her mother. Ah yes; the lovely Margaret. Well that would have been a normal kind of post traumatic experience day, but instead she had to deal with a bewildered time traveller. I was just assessing my chances of getting a little bit of lunch, when she walked into the bedroom.

"I have to go out to get Stevie from pre-school in a minute. Seeing's you're here, do you think you could go down to the kitchen and make us all some sandwiches for when we get back? We should try to keep things looking normal for him, don't you think?"

I could have cried and not just because of the

imminence of food. I had never forgotten the last words she'd said to me "last night", apart from "Go to hell!" She'd said "I did nothing but love you." I couldn't really argue with that, or fault her devotion to our marriage. Somehow, though, we didn't quite gel, but at this moment I would find it hard to put that forward in my defence: "I put my wife and child through the wringer, m'lud, because we didn't quite gel".

So I find myself in my old kitchen, trying to remember where we kept the knives and whether Carla would prefer cheese and tomato or ham and mustard. Outside, the blackbird, or a blackbird, has spotted Tiggy curled up asleep on the armchair just inside the living room window, and the noisy ear-bashing starts again. Is there no peace for the wicked? Or the cat?

I click the kettle on when I hear Carla open the door. She is clearly mildly amused about something:

"Stevie told one of the other kids that Daddy's hair was falling out, and I've had a couple of the mothers asking me if you're being treated for cancer. They were really concerned about us." Her grimace and raised eyebrows convey the message that cancer was the least of the things we were concerned about at the moment.

"What did you tell them?"

"Well since none of them have seen you I said he was exaggerating and that your barber had misunderstood your instructions. How we roared….."

Turns out the preferred sandwich was cheese and tomato: "but you know I always have a bit of lettuce and a sprinkling of salt!"

"Sorry! Can't think why I forgot that."

Stevie's done a picture for me. It's a family picture, in which he has skillfully captured my diminishing hair. Somehow he's contrived to make me look like a monk, but given that he only saw me like this for an hour or so this morning, I can't be too hard on him. Also, I know that his artistic leanings will blossom into a career as a talented graphic designer, but I'm not going to throw our relatively pleasant lunch into confusion by trying to explain how I know that.

I realise that Carla is staring at me. It's not the look of love, but I can understand that. It's a look of fear and concern.

"What if it is cancer?" she whispers, quiet for Stevie's benefit.

"It's not cancer."

"How do you know? It must be something pretty serious to cause this...this....deterioration overnight."

"Yes, it must be, but I feel like I'll last long enough to see the doctor tomorrow. Speaking of which, would you mind if I stayed here for one more night? I don't mind sleeping on the sofa or in the spare room."

"Oh. You're not going to find out how your, er, your, shall we say, significant other is? Won't you be missed?" The words suggested concern; the tone, not so much.

"No, I took the liberty of phoning while you were out and told her I'm too ill to drive over."

Lying comes naturally to some of us. And 1471 hadn't

been invented yet either.

"Well those are the only options then; the sofa or the spare room. You're certainly not sleeping with me."

I'm swamped by another wave of speculation; if I did sleep with my wife from whom I'm not yet divorced in 1991 when I'm already married to somebody that I won't meet for at least another fifteen years, does it still count as adultery? I suppose I could give it a shot and then ask Trisha what she thinks if I manage to get back. Best not, I think. I have to say, whoever is behind all this is really fucking with my head.

"And I've been thinking about that tee-shirt you were wearing. I still don't understand how you could have a shirt dated 2002. What's all that about?"

I've been thinking about that too, and the best makeshift answer I can come up with is,
"Oh, that Roger Waters! I think he gets a bit above himself sometimes. You know he sort of fell out with the rest of Pink Floyd, right? I think it's a spoof shirt, predicting a rosy future for himself."

Well I thought that was feasible, and not bad going at short notice, and it seems to work.

"I suppose she bought you that, did she? I've never seen it before!"

One step forward, one step back.

And so the long day wore on, a mixture of reminiscences and recriminations, and I have to say, unusually these days, I was quite looking forward to going to sleep.

The spare room wasn't quite guest ready, but once I'd shifted a few boxed jigsaw puzzles and the ironing basket, dug out a sleeping bag, I made myself tolerably comfortable. I missed my Sony headphones; would've blocked out the sobbing noises coming from the room next door. I'd lived through that once and hearing it again wasn't making me feel any better about myself.

I'd taken Stevie's picture to bed with me and had another look at it as I sat down on the edge of the bed. Expecting to see the monk-like caricature of myself that I'd seen before, it was a shock to find that the representation of me in his picture looked more like Klaus Kinski's Nosferatu. With what had been going on today, I suppose I should be relieved that I was already sitting down, but to be honest, with what had been going on today, I was starting to get used to somebody or something playing with reality. Or what passed for reality round here.

The next morning gives me the opportunity to slip out of the house early and hurry down to the market without having to fabricate another ruse for Carla's benefit. My route to the market stalls takes me, somewhat surprisingly, through an old shopping arcade, where my focus is distracted by a shop window displaying old toy cars. I notice the familiar blue and yellow of the Matchbox models in a glass display cabinet inside, so inside is where I go. What an amazing coincidence; the last two models I need to complete my collection, in the same shop, at the same time. A Harley-Davidson motorcycle with sidecar and a Jaguar Mark 2 are selling for £150 for the pair. If I stick them on my debit card I could finish my collection today.

I look around for somebody to serve me and an old man, whose gaunt and hook-nosed face seems somehow familiar, puts down his paper and comes over to see what I want. I indicate that I would like to purchase the two models I've seen, but he politely declines:

"I'm sorry Sir, but you can only have one."

"What do you mean? I have the money. I want them both!"

"Well you can't. You can only have one of them."

Utterly ridiculous! I walk out rather than waste any more time arguing with the intransigent old bastard. I should just have time for coffee and a bit of breakfast before I get to the market, so I deviate into a coffee shop and order a double espresso from the ancient barista, and decide on a BLT and a flapjack to go with it.

"Sorry Sir. You can only have one."

"What?!"

"You can have the BLT or the flapjack, but not both."

"What kind of a place is this, for crying out loud?"

I look around the coffee shop, which turns out to be Carla's spare room, where I'm lying on my back, feeling more than slightly jaded because the little bit of sleep I'd managed to enjoy last night was spoiled by another of my challenging dreams. The presence of the old man in the dream didn't really carry any significance to me while I was sleeping, but as I came fully awake it got through to me. I was starting to get very pissed off with all this manipulation and cryptic messages. And last night, he spoiled my son's picture. It's all getting a bit much.

Love Is The Drug

In her university days, Melanie had been a bit of a puzzle to her friends. While they were all into house music and raves in their spare time away from their educational activities, she seemed to them to be like a bit of a throwback to the nineteen-sixties. She generally stopped short of wearing flowers in her hair, but the beads and the kaftans and the cheesecloth shirts would have her acquaintances greeting her with tiresome expressions like "Peace, man" or "Are you turned on and tuned out today?" Tedious, man. But at least they had the frequent enjoyment of a bit of weed in common. Not only that, she could be persuaded to entertain them with some sort of mildly occult demonstration as she developed her keen interest in all things mystic. They'd all had her do Tarot card readings for them and were always amazed that she could find so much truth in the cards. The truth was, Melanie was a quick study and drew a lot of her information from observations and made logical predictions based on those. She wasn't entirely sure herself whether there was anything else guiding the readings.

Her boyfriend Greg was always impressed though. He was in his last year at uni when she was in her second and they'd met in the student bar where he worked occasional shifts pulling pints. He was a loud, life and soul of any party kinda guy and for some reason, more than likely the usual testosterone driven one, made it his mission to bring the markedly quieter and shy Melanie out of her shell. Most people were noticeably quieter than Greg, but that didn't put her off, opposites attract being a cliché for a reason, and her friends eventually got used to the incongruous pairing of the rugby player and the hippy.

One of their crowd lived not far away at Hebden Bridge and so when they had a free weekend a small group of them would take the train from Leeds down the Calderdale line and spend a couple of nights at his big house if his parents were away. Actually, Melanie was quite happy if his parents were there, because she discovered that they had an extensive library of books on occult subjects. Her friend's mother, Joyce, was more than happy to talk to Melanie about them and about the artefacts she had collected over the years.

Melanie's access to all this reading material fuelled her fascination with the darker side of magic. Greg would tell his friends that you never knew what you were going to get with Mel; beads and flowers or crucifixes and pentagrams. The Divine Ms R he called her.

The routine of university life and the distractions of mysticism and magic were abruptly interrupted when she received a message in the autumn of 1991, telling her that her beloved cousin, Yvonne, had died as a result of a drug overdose.

Melanie was devastated. She and Yvonne were at least a decade apart in age, but her older cousin used to be her babysitter and they had become very fond of each other. Yvonne was the sister she'd never had, and they treated each other like they were sisters. She was the shoulder to cry on when her boyfriend, who'd promised to love her always, had dumped her for that cow Sharon. A shoulder to cry on is important when you're thirteen. Yvonne was there for the shopping trips and for blagging her way into bars and clubs when she was only sixteen. And she let Mel use her Ford Fiesta when she was learning to drive. But just lately their lives had gone in different directions, with Yvonne working up in Sunderland and Melanie having got her A levels and gone off to university in Leeds.

She'd gleaned through the family grapevine that Yvonne had been involved with a married man. Yvonne was always in and out of love with somebody, but couldn't seem to find somebody to really make her happy, that was the impression Melanie got. From conversations the two of them had recently, Mel felt that Yvonne had found someone really special, but she had been a bit cagey about details for some reason. Perhaps she thought Melanie would disapprove of him being married. The older members of the family certainly did and had predicted that no good ever came of that sort of thing, and the word circulating now was that they were proved right, in the worst possible way for Yvonne and for the family. Melanie's father had spoken to his niece's friend Sheila, and she pulled no punches in her condemnation of Yvonne's lover. Melanie determined to find out more about this man. If this Sheila person was right, he would be made to pay.

I've Made An Appointment

I'm an early riser usually, especially if I have a big day ahead of me. I had a feeling today was going to be one of those, one way or the other. Putting aside for a moment the implications of last night's dream, whatever they were, I picked a few items of clothing to wear from my nineties' collection.

I didn't know what kind of reception I would get from Carla this morning, but I doubted there would be an entirely comfortable atmosphere. Being caught out in infidelity can make you feel like a stranger in your own home; being away for twenty seven years means you are, most definitely, a stranger in your own home.

I made my way quietly to the bathroom and when I came out Carla was in the kitchen, boiling water to make coffee; two cups, I was kind of gratified to see. It felt like a cease fire had been declared, but you never knew when a breakdown in diplomacy would have the bullets flying again.

"If you're moving your stuff today, you're going to need the car. You haven't said where it is yet."

Damn! I hadn't thought of a lie to cover that yet. I've had all night too.

"That's because I can't actually remember. Hopefully the walk to the surgery and back might jog my memory."

"Look Chris, the car's no big deal. It'll turn up, or the police can find it. But this thing that's happened to you, whatever it is you've got; are you sure you're going to be looked after properly if you go to........you know what I mean?"

This looks very much like an undeserved olive branch. The hostile looks I've been on the receiving end of lately have been replaced, at least for a moment, with a show of concern, but there's pain there too. That's not something the young Chris stuck around to see back in 1991, but now I'm here, experiencing the early consequences of my actions and with the full knowledge of what they will lead to in the future, both for Carla and for our son.

Did I do the wrong thing? Would I do the same thing again? I can't deal with these big questions right now. The best way to deal with a potentially painful exchange is to deflect her attention in the direction of the anticipated business of the day.

"I can't think about that right now; I have to get myself to the doctor's and find out what's causing me to look like this. Might be beyond the scope of our local GP, but I have to start somewhere. So if you don't mind, I'd better get ready and go; I managed to get an early appointment. I'll come back for my stuff."

I knew I wasn't going to be coming back for my stuff, nor would I be seeing Carla or Stevie again, at least not as the twenty seven year aged and matured me. I wondered if I should say some kind of goodbye, but I'd left without saying goodbye once before, so I'm sure I could manage it again; callous bastard. But then what would I say? "Well cheerio then. Take care of yourself.'"? In my absence, taking care of herself was something she'd have to do anyway.

I was earnestly hoping that she wasn't going to volunteer to come with me, because I had no intention of going anywhere near the doctor. I didn't think he'd have anything to treat Coercive Time Travel Syndrome, or whatever it is I've been maliciously afflicted with. I had to remind myself that this scenario I found myself in was, I believed, some kind of skilfully constructed fake and I very keenly desired to find out who the designer was and why they had gone to all this trouble.

Could It Be Magic?

Very few people are prepared to follow their vengeful thoughts to the point of carrying out acts of violence. The rules of civilised society usually put paid to that. Even if the perpetration of such acts seem justifiable, there is a balancing fear of the consequences, whether they are physical, moral or judicial. Melanie Robinson was extremely frustrated by the constraints of this reasoning. By the November of 1991 all she had been able to do was find out the name of the man she blamed for her cousin's death and that he worked for the same car hire company that Yvonne had, but he'd left the local area. There must be some way he could be made to suffer for screwing with Yvonne's head to the extent that she killed herself. No; Melanie couldn't accept that the Yvonne she knew, or thought she knew, would deliberately take her own life.

But this Chris whatever-his-name-is was responsible, she was sure of it, just because he couldn't be bothered to drive over to prevent her death. He'd admitted as much to Yvonne's friend Sheila. At least he'd admitted that Yvonne had phoned him, but he hadn't taken her seriously. Well it's pretty fucking serious now, was Melanie's thought, and she determined that she was going to find a way to make him pay. Her initial anger-fuelled designs of murder and mutilation had passed as common sense prevailed; she lacked the skill set anyway. Wasn't there a saying that revenge is a dish best served cold? Perhaps if capital punishment wasn't an option, then a lifetime of misery could be arranged.

Melanie confided as much to her friend's mum, Joyce, on one of her weekend visits to Hebden Bridge. Melanie seemed to be spending as much time, if not more, in Joyce's library of occult books as she did hanging out with Greg and the others. It was good to have somebody to talk to about her feelings who didn't think she was overreacting. Greg had offered to "go and fill him in" if she found out where he lived, but that didn't seem a very satisfactory solution and besides, Greg was all talk, a gentle giant who confined his acts of violence to the rugby pitch.

Joyce, moreover, was enthralled by her young visitor's interest in her favourite subject and her response to Melanie's observation that it was a pity they couldn't just punish him with magic was "Who said we can't?"

"You're kidding, right?"

Joyce's face suggested she wasn't kidding.

"Are you serious?"

"Yes, I'm serious, Melanie. But I need to know how serious you are, because magic isn't something to play about with. I'm not talking Paul Daniels type magic here. It's the real thing."

"The real thing. What? Real magic? So what are you saying? Witchcraft? Evil spirits? That sort of thing?"

"If you could find somebody to sort out the man you've told me about, would you call them evil? That would be well deserved justice surely."

"Yeah, I guess that's the way I see it. But what? Are you saying you can do this?"

"Look, Mel. This has to stay between us, okay. What I do isn't for the entertainment of your silly friends. I'm prepared to share this with you because I think you'd take it seriously. Am I right?"

"Yes, I mean, of course. Wow! How long have you been into this, this kind of magic?"

"Oh, since I was about your age; so a good thirty years or so."

"And what does Trevor think about it?"

"He'd certainly laugh if he knew about it. No, my husband just thinks it's a harmless fascination, a collection of books and ornaments for me to dust, as harmless as making jam for the W.I., and I'm quite happy to keep him thinking that."

"Uh huh….so what are you then, some sort of white witch? Or the other sort?"

"Not any sort of witch, no. I like to think of myself as an enabler, a provider, a conduit between a spirit world and the human world."

"Are you telling me that you can….actually I don't want to guess what you're telling me!"

"I'm telling you that I think I can find somebody who may agree to help you with your problem, but he's, how should I put it? Not exactly local."

"Oh come on! You can't mean not exactly local in the sense that he's….."

"Out of this world. Yes, you catch on fast. Still interested?"

"I'm intrigued! So what do we have to do?"

"Not today. Go back to hanging out with your friends tonight, but find some pretext to come over here by yourself as soon as you can. Meanwhile, I'll try to set up a contact for you for when you come back."

"You make it sound like a job interview. I was imagining some kind of ceremony with candles and chanting."

"Not with the individual I'm thinking of. He can't be bothered with all that what he calls children's party nonsense. He's not your typical demon."

"Demon! Jesus Christ! What are you getting me into here?"

"Like I told you; somebody who's good at sorting out people who've managed to avoid the justice they deserve."

"How do you know he's good? Are you saying you've had previous experience of what he does?"

"Oh yes! I had a rather pathetic ex-boyfriend who has to be helped to feed himself now.

"Good grief! You're a dark horse alright. You don't look like the sort of person who'd be into any sort of extreme revenge. What did this demon do to him, for God's sake?"

"I didn't find out the details, and Mr Formerly-Super-Confident-Casanova never ever talked about it to anybody. Job done though."

"And what does this demon get out of it? I mean, is he going to demand my first-born child or something?"

"Oh don't be silly. You've been reading too many horror stories for my liking. No, he'll just do it if he likes your idea, if he likes you, out of the goodness of his heart. I'm not sure if goodness and heart are the right words where he's concerned, but he's like, well you've probably seen Edward Woodward in The Equaliser? Like that, only from another world."

"So I was right. I will have to do an interview. I hate interviews."

"But you'll do it, yes? Shall I see if I can arrange the meeting, or interview if you like?"

Melanie, with very mixed feelings, agreed to Joyce's proposal. On her way home to Leeds she kept telling herself, in the cold light of the railway carriage, that the idea was preposterous, that Joyce wasn't quite as sound in the head as she would have people believe, that demons are fiction. She must have been drinking or smoking too much when she had that conversation with Joyce and long before she arrived back at her flat she decided that she would call the house at Hebden Bridge as soon as she could get to a payphone and no doubt she and Joyce would have a good laugh about the whole thing.

But when she phoned the next day it was to find that Joyce had already set things in motion:

"He says he'll see you tomorrow morning, here, in the library. I gave him the brief outline of what you told me and he said it might be fun to do something about it if he wasn't too busy."

"Fun?" Melanie couldn't see the funny side, but nevertheless she found herself back on the Calderdale train the next morning, having feigned illness to skip the morning's lecture. Joyce met her at the door and led her through to the library.

"You look terrified, dear. I can understand that, but there's no need to be. He won't bite, although his manners aren't always of the highest standard I've noticed. Or at least a bit unconventional. I'll introduce you and then you can tell him what it is you want doing."

"Are you going to stay with me? Please?"

"That depends on him really. He might decide to order me out."

"Great! Err...what does he look like?"

"Oh nothing scary. No horns or tail. This time round he's like a little grumpy old man. So are you ready to meet Mr E?"

"You're having me on? Mr E? Mystery? Is that his name?"

"He's never told me his name. That's just what I call him. So he'll answer to it, but I don't think he's very happy about it. Too corny! Don't tell him I told you. Ready?"

It's ....er.... Mr E

"Just follow me, dear." Joyce knocks quietly then opens the door and, as instructed, Melanie follows, not knowing exactly what to expect, having never met a demon before. She didn't imagine, however, that they were all like the diminutive old man that was sitting behind the library's desk with his head in his hands. With her first look at this unimpressive figure it occurred to her that she'd only got Joyce's word for it that the individual she'd come all the way out from Leeds to meet was a demon. He looked like a retired accountant who'd fallen on hard times and had come to interview for a job as part-time gardener. He looked very ordinary, and everything else in the room looked very ordinary, that's if you were willing to overlook the pentagram chalked on the floor and the fragments of a broken urn or vase scattered within its outlines. There was a lot of ash too, some of it amongst the pieces of pottery, some of it on the old man's black coat.

"Joyce! At last!" His voice was harsh, as if he'd inhaled a good portion of the ash. "Fetch me a clothes brush. I can't receive visitors looking like this."

Joyce immediately turns to fetch a brush.

"You're not going to leave me with him already are you?" Melanie whispers as Joyce makes to pass her.

"No need to worry, young lady. I'm not going to eat you. Stopped doing that sort of thing years ago, although, I have to say, you look good enough to eat. Manna from heaven, as the Good Book says. Joyce was right about you, I can see. A very pretty thing indeed."

Melanie's inner feminist shoves its way to the front, pushing her fear to one side:
"I didn't come here to be ogled by a man old enough to be my grandfather!"

"Ha! Like it. I'm old enough to be your grandfather's grandfather, if you must know. If Methusalah had a grandfather, I'd've been him."

"Whatever. You just look like a dirty old man."

"Oh do I? Haven't had time to freshen up. Sorry about that. I'll be less dirty when Joyce comes back with a brush. Ah, here she is."

He busies himself with the brush, while Melanie stands watching him and wondering if this is anything but a waste of time and thinks about the lecture notes she would have to borrow when she got back to Leeds. The old man, alleged demon, appears to have completely lost interest in her. He is leafing through a Bible which he has extracted from the recesses of his coat.

"Jared; that was it."

"What are you talking about?"

"It wasn't me. It was Jared."

"What was Jared?"

"Not what. Who. Jared was Methusalah's grandfather, not me. Jared begat Enoch, Enoch begat Methusalah, it says here. Although how much we can believe that I don't know. It says Jared was one hundred and sixty two when he fathered Enoch, so either men were really men in those days, or women had very low standards, or somebody's got their sums wrong."

He looks up at the two blank faces.

"I just like to get things right, but if you're not interested we'll move on to the business of the day. Now then; Miss Melanie Robinson I believe, yes? Or do you prefer Ms? Never mind. I don't care either way. What can I do for you? I presume you have a valid reason for summoning me into this world. Apparently there is a time for everything under the sun, I seem to recall reading somewhere, but mine's valuable and I don't take kindly to having it wasted, so what is it you want?"

Melanie is somewhat discouraged by his switching from sleazy to gentlemanly politeness to veiled threat, in the space of less than a minute. He may look old, but there is steel in his voice and a penetrating strength in his eyes. And his eyes; do retired accountants have purple eyes? She summons up the courage to tell him why she's there, but then says something she immediately wishes she hadn't:

"Did you just come out of that vase?"

"What?!" he roars. "Joyce, who is this child? Next she'll be asking me to grant her three wishes."

"Please be patient with her; she's a little bit nervous. If you remember, I was too, the first time we met."

"True, yes. You were, and if I remember correctly you asked me about the three wishes as well, as if I were a mere genie. Genies! They're like game show hosts. Very low brow."

"And you said I could only have one, so, please; give her a break."

His anger subsides; "As you wish, Joyce. Your mild answer has turned away my rage. That's in the book of Proverbs. There's some good stuff there. And Ecclesiastes. Have a look some time. But young Melanie; forgive me. You wanted to ask me something. Go on."

"Very sorry Mr…"

"Don't say it!"

"Err, very sorry. Joyce tells me you're a vengeance demon."

"Does she now? Yes, I remember that bit of work I did for you, Joyce. How is the poor chap? Still being spoon fed by his mother I understand. So, yes, Miss Robinson, I suppose you could call me a vengeance demon. I prefer to say that I work in the field of creative consequences and remedial repercussions. Hmm?….CC…RR. I like the alliteration. No? Just me then. Never mind. Be that as it may, you need to tell me some details about whoever has caused you sufficient upset to risk waking me up."

Again, she thought, that bit of threat. Nevertheless;

"A couple of months ago, my cousin Yvonne killed herself with a drink and drugs overdose. Her bastard of a boyfriend could've stopped her, but he didn't."

"Dearie me! Did he just stand and watch?"

"No! He just didn't bother to go and help when she phoned him to tell him what she was doing."

"How do you know she phoned him if she's dead? Did she leave a note?"

"No she didn't, but he told her friend Sheila that Yvonne had called him."

"So if she didn't leave a note it may have been an accident."

"It may have been, but that's not the point, is it? He should have gone to help her and he didn't. Unforgivable!"

"Well you clearly think so."

"Too right I do. This lowlife had been cheating on his wife for years apparently, then Yvonne gets herself mixed up with him and now she's dead."

"Enemies erased. Hurting the hurtful."

"What?"

"Forgive me. Your story was starting to bore me, so I was just thinking up some more snappy phrases to promote my service. But honestly, it all sounds very mundane to me. Do you not have the imagination to deal with it yourself? Couldn't you just go and pour paint-stripper on his car or poison his cat?"

"I knew this was a waste of time, Joyce. Who is this guy? How do I even know he's what you say he is. Looks like a washed up oldie to me."

Instantly the room goes cold and dark; there's a noise and thundering vibration as if the Calder Valley line had diverted through the house. Intermittent light flashes, and Melanie has the sensation of being lifted further off the floor every time the room lights up. She felt as if her breath was being sucked out of her. In the brief gaps between the moments of intense darkness she is horrified to find herself sitting behind the desk and Joyce pinned against the ceiling by a huge black hand. Shrouded in smoke or mist, the creature at the other end of the arm was huge, an indistinct shape, but something like the Incredible Hulk's big brother.

And just as suddenly, everything and everybody was back where they started.

"Mel, I did say try not to upset him." Joyce attempts to sort out her bedraggled hair and clothes, the only obvious sign that something out of the ordinary had happened.

"So, young lady; happy now?" The vengeance demon is back at the desk, his old man persona once again in place. Melanie thought that if he'd put on a display like that in the first place she wouldn't have questioned his credentials, and, once she'd plucked up enough courage to speak again, said as much.

"I take your point, but I find it doesn't put my interviewees in a particularly relaxed frame of mind if I start like that. I would have thought that was obvious. What are you studying at university? I hope it's not psychology." Melanie debated rising to the bait, but then decided against risking another display of annoyance. The demon consults a sheet of paper in a loose-leaf folder that Melanie is sure wasn't there two minutes earlier.

"While you were no doubt being impressed by the recent small sample of my abilities, I was doing a bit of research into the background of your sad story. You were unaware, it appears, that your cousin's friend Sheila was the one who suggested the stunt with the paracetamols. Would you like me to give her some attention as well? Although, hang on, hang on," and he refers to another sheet of paper, "it seems she's going to finish up laden with credit card debts, working for an insurance company's call centre and will be regularly abused by her alcoholic husband, so I don't see the point really, do you? Indeed, it is written, whatever a man, or in this case a woman, is sowing, this he, or in this case she, will also reap"

Joyce interrupts; "What's with all the Bible quotations? I've never heard you talk like that before. A bit out of character, if you don't mind me saying."

"Ah yes, that. A little project I started recently; a sort of "know your enemy" strategy. I had to draw the line at the "vengeance is mine saith the Lord" concept, otherwise I'd be stifling my talents. But there are some cracking one-liners in there amongst all the holier than thou and everybody else nonsense. Apologies if you're of a religious bent Miss Robinson"

"Not especially. But what you said means you can see into the future too?"

"Of course, but only if I choose to. Otherwise I'd never be able to enjoy watching a film or reading a book. Cape Fear's on at the cinema this week and I'm keen to see De Niro being really unpleasant. Fancy going? My treat. At my age, I can get in cheap on Tuesday afternoons. No? But I suppose what you meant is you want me to tell you how this Mr Adwell is going to turn out, didn't you?" A third sheet of paper: "Looks to me like he does rather well for himself. Hmmm! I understand you've recently considered the old saying that revenge is a dish best served cold."

Melanie is a little offended, but hardly surprised, that he's been reading her mind too.

"Don't alarm yourself; I'm not a read and tell type of demon. Your opinions of Greg's table manners are safe with me. No, I was thinking about the cold dish thing. Are you perhaps prepared to play a long game? A really long game."

"How do you mean, long? I've been thinking about this for a couple of months already."

"I was thinking more like years. Catch him when he's at his most comfortable and prosperous and not expecting any reprisals. I've always found this a most satisfying approach. Ah! You look disappointed."

"Years? I don't call that satisfying."

"Well that's my best offer. Or do it yourself. Of course, if you had the nous you'd have done it by now. Like I said before, it's not a very interesting story, and I'm a busy demon. Purveyor of purgatory. Hmmm. Yes, I like that one. But here's an idea; something you might do for yourself. Get close to this Adwell fellow if you can. Inveigle or smarm your way into his life if you feel like it. Infiltrate; better word I think. Then you'll have a ringside seat when the fun starts, you see. I'm thoughtful like that; I wouldn't want you to miss anything. Now go; leave me alone. Live long and prosper."

"That's not the Bible; that's from Star Trek."

Fancy A Coffee?

I managed to get out of the house by a quarter to nine with the declared intention of walking to the surgery. My first priority, however, was to get to the local newsagent's and see if the papers had anything to say about the missing Patricia Hallam, or whether it was only in the paper I'd been reading. I was probably being targeted with tailor made fake news, but who knew what might be happening in this very twisted version of my history? There was obviously a distinct risk that I might bump into people that knew me, but I was prepared for that:

"Chris?" ventured the newsagent warily.

"Ah sorry, no. I'm his Uncle Andy. People often say he looks like me."

"Blimey. They're not wrong. Well tell him I was asking after him when you see him. He's a canny lad is Chris."

Unsolicited testimonials are great. The papers divulged no new information about Trisha, which is what I had expected really, so my only course was to walk to the town centre and try to find this elusive old man. I occasionally pass people I think I recognise, and some of them clearly think there's something familiar about me, but I'm in no mood to stop and put them wise to who I am. My mind is in turmoil. I haven't yet managed to sort out my priorities. Can I find a way to save Yvonne from her self-inflicted demise? Can I definitely rule out the possibility that the young Trisha has been abducted or kidnapped or just disappeared? I can't be absolutely sure, although it sure is adding to my stress; absolutely. I just want to be home in my comfortable future that I used to know, with my loving wife, my morning coffee ritual and my hardware store. I'll never complain about stocktaking again.

I realise that getting back home is my priority and that just makes me feel like a completely selfish shit. Getting back to my comfort zone is more important than trying to save Yvonne. I didn't take her seriously the first time round, and this time round I'm no better. I just want my life to be normal again, whatever normal is when I've been through an experience nobody's going to believe. If I see Trisha again, will she believe me? "Those dreams I've been having……"

This is giving me a headache, and I'm worried about the mixed blessing of finally confronting the person whom I feel certain holds the key to all this trauma. I don't foresee an amiable chat. And I'm also agitated by the thought that, if he's not there, I don't have a clue what to do next. It's not like we have an appointment. I suppose if he's not there I could go to the doctor and throw myself on the mercy of the medical profession. I'll probably need medical help at that point.

It took me half an hour to reach the edge of the town's market square. The stalls were grouped according to the kind of produce they sold. You don't want the fishmongers next to the frocks and tee shirts. I figured that a flower seller might not be too far from the fruit and veg, and then suddenly I saw him.

He'd seen me first, and I knew at once that he'd been expecting me. The bastard! I couldn't believe that this bald, wrinkly, skinny little octogenarian could be the instigator of so much trouble in my life, awake or asleep. Perhaps I should approach with caution; a bald, wrinkly, skinny little octogenarian with enough power to create a detailed mock-up of my life and who knows what other abilities. This was the man from the model shop and the coffee shop, and the SS guard on the train that I'd seen in my dreams. Now he's standing at a flower stall, smirking at me. Smirking is a real wind-up, isn't it?

I paused and just stared at him, but then resumed walking until we were in conversational distance. He spoke first:

"I'm wondering if I should say it."

"Say what, for God's sake?"

"Ah, Mr Adwell; I've been expecting you."

"You think this is funny?"

"I do, actually. But then I'm not you, am I? Not at the sharp end, so to speak."

I lost it a bit at that. So much for approaching with caution. My confusion and frustration gave way to anger and I lunged forward and grabbed him by the lapels of his long black coat.

"Look, you little shit......."

Now, I should have thought that this kind of behaviour in a busy market place in the middle of the morning is bound to attract attention. A middle aged six footer beating up a very much shorter eighty year old is not socially acceptable, and cries of astonishment and disapproval were ringing out. I eased my grip a little, and then felt a hand on the back of my jacket; a hand at the end of the long arm of the law.

"Everything alright here, sir?" Seemed a strange question, what with the look of rage on my face, but I suppose he was trying to calm things down to a level where I would come quietly. Again, the "flower seller" spoke first:

"It's alright, officer. We're just rehearsing a play." Good one!

"Is that so?" I went along with this, and added an unrehearsed line:

"Yes, officer, but I can see that this probably isn't the best time and place to do it. Sorry about that."

"Very true, sir. Now if you don't want to be done for conduct likely to cause a breach of the peace, I suggest you take it somewhere a little more private."

"Extremely sorry, officer," and producing a couple of bits of printed card from the depths of one of his pockets, the old man, or whatever he was, continued, "And please, accept a couple of these complimentary tickets to the matinee performance at the town hall next Saturday. Perhaps you and your good lady would enjoy the show."
Throughout all this, with or without my hands on his lapels, he'd never lost the smirk on his face. After the policeman had left us he said,
"I wouldn't do that again if I were you."

"What do you mean? That sounds like a threat."

"Good. That was my intention. I have powers that you cannot comprehend. Hmm. That sounded needlessly dramatic, I think, don't you? I purvey purgatory. No; doesn't really work. Let's try, I don't just do tricks with impromptu theatre tickets."

"Are you trying to tell me you can do me serious physical harm?"

"Exactly. Well, I think so. It's been a long time since I've had to. I may be a bit rusty, but yes; you've got the gist, but lately I've been trying to apply the peaceful answer that turns away rage."

"Right, okay! Thanks for the warning, but why are you doing this?" I kept my voice down, my words coming through gritted teeth so as not to attract any more attention. "Why have you completely fucked up my life? First you invade my dreams, then you creep about in my real life, and then you take me back in time. I assume it's you, yes?"

He nods his assent.

"Yes, but it's nothing personal."

"Nothing personal! What do you mean, nothing personal? It certainly feels very bloody personal. And have you done something to my wife? That thing in my newspaper…"

"Like I said, nothing personal. I'm just doing my job."

"What?! What kind of a job is that?"

"Look, why don't we do what our recent policeman acquaintance suggested and take this somewhere a little less public? Can I buy you a coffee? You can have as many as you like this time."

Still seething, and infuriated by his manner, which bordered on insolence, I supposed I had no option but to go along with him if I wanted to get any answers. Besides, I could do with a decent cup of coffee; Carla's instant wasn't to my liking any more.

So we set off to find a coffee shop, an unlikely pair of companions to behold, even if anybody beholding us was unaware that we were a reluctant, worried time traveller and his tormentor. I still felt very out of control of the whole situation and had no idea how to change that. I didn't take kindly to being a passenger in my own life, which just added to the long list of things I wasn't currently taking kindly to.

The coffee shop was busy, as one would expect on a market day. It hardly seemed any more private than the market, but at least that would discourage my lapel-grabbing activities and whatever unholy retribution my new drinking partner claimed he could unleash.

We found a vacant table and slid into our seats. I'd ordered a double espresso, with designs on a second one when that was finished. Well he did say I could. And a Chelsea bun; I didn't really feel like eating, but if he was paying…..

"Right! I want some answers. What do you mean, you're just doing your job? Seems like a pretty fucked-up way to make a living to me."

"Oh I don't do it to make a living. It's more like somewhere between a hobby and a calling. I would say I'm a benefactor."

I almost accidentally sprayed him with my first mouthful of coffee when he said that.

"Benefactor! I don't feel like a beneficiary!"

"Not you, sir. My clients are the beneficiaries. I carry out their instructions."

"Right! All this shit that's been happening to me, somebody put you up to it? Who was it? Who wants to give me all this grief? What have I done to deserve this?"

"Sorry Mr Adwell; my code of practice prevents me from revealing my clients' names."

"Oh please, call me Chris, why don't you!" I can do a nice line in sarcasm when the occasion calls for it. "Well it's great to know that your client has the services of such a professional. So fucking discreet! God Almighty! If not who, then why?"

"Perhaps you could temper your language, sir. I'm not at all happy with it. Although I don't mind you taking the Lord's name in vain; he thinks way too much of himself anyway."

He clearly wasn't happy with the long chain of expletives I put together at that request. I wound them up with a repetition of, "What have I done to deserve this? My life's so undramatically normal and comfortable, I can't think of anybody being offended by what I do. Well, that was my life until you came along."

"I think that's part of the problem, sir. I don't think it's what you're actually doing now; more like, in the words of my client, you seem to have got away with murder."

"What? I haven't murdered anybody."

"It was meant metaphorically, I believe. Although, if I check your file, I believe I'm correct in saying, there was an unfortunate death some years ago. Yes, it's right here."

While we were talking he had extracted a folder from the inside pocket of his coat and proceeded to open it on the table between us. But at the mention of the word death my heart missed a beat. He must be referring to Yvonne. Where the hell did he get that information? Then again, if he could invade my dreams and transport me through time, putting a file together would be simple. I realised he was staring intently at me, with a finger poised above a line of writing in the folder he had produced. What else was going to come out of that coat?

"You see, Mr Adwell, according to my client, you haven't exactly enjoyed a particularly blameless past. It's all here in your file. You were unfaithful to your wife in 1986 and then again in 1991. You left her for another woman, whom you let down in the worst way possible. You let her die."

"Now hang on! I made a mistake there, I admit. But I thought she was bluffing."

"Obviously she wasn't so, yes, a big mistake. And then you just moved well away, swept it all under the carpet, and simply left your wife to bring up your son without very much in the way of help from you. How very noble."

"Where are you getting all this crap from? Because that's not how it was from my point of view. And why now? Why wait all this time?"

"Sorry. I've been too busy to fit you in. Anyway, like I said, this is the information I received from my client, but it's not necessarily my opinion. I feel it may be a little biased, but I did accept the assignment and so I've carried it out."

"And that was to make my life hell was it? As if I haven't done that to myself already over the years. Why are you looking at me like that?"

"I was just thinking that it's not often I get to sit down and have a chat with my victims. Usually I've driven them mad or they've at least had some sort of mental collapse by now. You seem to be hanging on quite well in my opinion."

"Thank you. Bloody hell; why am I saying thank you to you? I'm only holding it together because I have to believe I can get back to my own time and now, do I need to find Trisha as well? Or is that bit not real? God, this is confusing."

"Oh yes, that bit's real. She's here, just like you are."

"Why? What has this got to do with her?"

"Nothing directly. But then if it adds to your problems, it's a job well done, wouldn't you say?"

"You twisted bastard," I almost shouted, almost grabbed the front of his coat again, before I remembered the legal and potentially catastrophic implications of assaulting him.

"Language, please! There's no rush; all in good time, Chris. You did say I could call you Chris, yes? First tell me how you think you've suffered. I'm interested."

"Why?"

"Let me tell you something. When I was first asked to take you on I can't say that I was very impressed with the brief. I mean a couple of affairs, an unfortunate death, a family abandoned; it's all a bit run of the mill. Happens all the time. Hardly worthy of a being of my talents, but she was very insistent, my client. Made out you were the spawn of the Devil. I have to say I've met the spawn of the Devil and you're nothing like them. You seem like a decent chap really."

"She? You said she."

"Damn! I knew I'd slip up."

"Yvonne had a friend who gave me a right ear-bashing. Was it her?"

"No it wasn't. But that's all I'm saying. You were going to tell me about how your life's been hell, to quote your words. Carry on, or you'll never find your wife."

"Are you offering me some kind of a deal here? I tell you whatever it is that you want to hear and you'll help me find Trisha?"

"Deal? Possibly. I'm still under contract to make you suffer, you understand, but I do have other interests and places to be. If you can convince me you've suffered enough I'll just tell my client the job's done and I can move on to some more deserving cases." He checks his paperwork again. "As I thought; it's not as if she wanted you dead."

"Oh well that's a consolation; driven half crazy, but not dead. You expect me to talk, not to die. Ha! Well thank her for me, won't you. And if I'm going to talk, I'll need some more coffee."

"Like that one, you mean?"

I look down and my cup contains a fresh double espresso.

"Very impressive, but won't there be some rule about consuming your own food on the premises?"

"Very droll, sir. I'm so glad to see you getting your sense of humour back. Anyway, go on. I'm all ears."

I looked up from my coffee to check if he actually was. With his talents it wouldn't have surprised me if he had been.

"How did you do that? The coffee, I mean."

"Oh that. I got the idea from that water into wine party trick that the so called son of God was supposed to have done. He started with water, but I only had an empty cup to work with. Ha! Would you prefer a cappuccino?"

"Tempting, but no; so get behind me Satan, if we're into Bible references now."

"Oh don't say that! You're mixing me up with someone else. I said that once; learned a thing or two about pecking orders that day, believe me. Now, back to your story. I haven't got all day."

"Where do I start? So much has happened in the last twenty four hours or so. It's been a horrifying experience."

"Why? Did you not enjoy meeting your ex wife and your son? He showed early promise of being artistic, didn't he?"

"Yes, and thanks for buggering up his picture."

"Just a little joke, sir. I do find this all very amusing, as I said."

"You knew just how to stick the knife in, didn't you? Dumped me right back in a scene that I hadn't lived through before; my home, the day after I left. So, did I enjoy meeting them? Bittersweet, really. Generally pretty uncomfortable, given the circumstances. And I scared the hell out of Carla. But, on the flip side, I remember thinking that most people only have photos of their kids. I had the opportunity to actually see him again in the flesh."

"Thanks to me!"

"Oh yeah, thanks a million! It just reminded me of everything I'd lost by not being there to see him grow up every day, only this time I was burdened with the knowledge of exactly how his life had turned out anyway. But you knew that, didn't you? All very amusing I'm sure. Well you needn't have bothered 'cos I've been beating myself up about it for twenty seven years already. After all I've seen here I'll probably be doing it for the next twenty seven too."

"Are you trying to tell me that all of my fine efforts were for nothing? I hate that!"

"Well I'm sure you'll be gratified to know that I'm super stressed out. I don't know how I got here, I don't know how to get back, I don't know what you've done with my wife and I don't know if I should try to save

Yvonne, because if I do I might never meet my wife! It all adds up to one giant head-fuck, and if you don't like the language then….then; no, I can't think of a better way to put it."

"No, as much as I disapprove of the expression, I can't either."

"Oh good! A tiny victory. So I failed at my marriage, even though it probably wasn't the ideal one for either of us; I still failed. I hate failure. And yes, I moved well away to take the pressure off, so I could have my nervous breakdown in peace! But I wasn't there for Stevie and when Carla remarried, well Stevie's new stepfather was a nice enough bloke, but he got to do all the things that I should've been doing."

"I have to say that you humans never cease to amaze me. You surrender willingly to your carnal desires, even though you know it always ends in pain for somebody. Whatever a man soweth, as the Quite Good Book says; I'm sure you know the rest."

"Yes, I know the rest and I'm certainly reaping now. But no, I can't argue with that. We give ourselves enough grief without your help. But here you are, having fun at my expense."

"Hmm…fun's probably a funny way of putting it, but I do always find it fascinating to see how you react if I apply a little pressure."

"I'm not a bloody lab rat!" This comes out loud enough to turn a few heads at nearby tables, and I get the impression that the man behind the counter is wondering if the sale of a coffee and a Chelsea bun is the most profitable use of the table we're occupying. As if he's reading my mind, which he probably is, my inquisitor gets up and goes to the counter and buys a cheese and tomato sandwich. He comes back, with a curiously smug look on his face, and places it in front of me.

"Eat that. You've got a big day in front of you."

"I have? And what are you looking so pleased about? Just because you can tell I'm hungry without asking?"

"Oh that bit's easy. No, there's a discount for pensioners on market day. He's bringing me a pot of tea in a minute."

He's really enjoying this. Who'd have thought that a cut price pot of tea would make a demon happy? And he's clearly aware of my anxiety, because he says,

"I can tell you're keen to move on and find the lovely Trisha, but there's no rush; she's not in any real danger, and I'm not letting this tea go to waste. So eat your sandwich and tell me about Yvonne. Obviously I'd prefer it if you don't talk with your mouth full. Very bad manners."

"It's so nice to meet a vengeance demon with high standards of table etiquette. Jesus! What do you want to know about Yvonne?"

"My client blames you for her death. Do you blame yourself?"

It seems a bit hypocritical that he can noisily slurp his tea when I can't talk with my mouth full, but I let it go. My thoughts are suddenly back with the trauma of discovering that my lover was dead, the intensity of the affair, the deceit at home, the nervous breakdown, the selfish escape to get away from all the reminders; they're all mixed up together.

"Yes, I do. And like I said already, I've been beating myself up about it for years. I'll never know whether she meant to die; God, it's hard to say that. Or if it was a repeat of her earlier plan gone horribly wrong. But the very few people I've talked to about it always say guilt's such a negative emotion, you have to move on, you can't turn the clock back, blah, blah, blah. So I nod and agree with them, and I've really tried to put it all behind me and convince myself to move on. Great! And then you come along and you really do turn the clock back."

"Yes I did. I've been fascinated by the results. I'm reminded of the trials of Job. You've read about him? That was an interesting experiment in applied torment. I know," the demon holds up a hand in a calming gesture as I start to rise from my seat in anger, "Not a lab rat, you said. But all those things you could change now you're here in your past, all those guilty feelings you could wipe away; your failed marriage, your adulteries, your lover's death, your little boy's future. Why don't you put it all right? Make everybody happy again, eh?"

For the first time in quite a while I smiled; a humourless effort: "I can't and you know it. This is all part of your twisted punishment, isn't it? All that stuff in my dream about "You can only have one". You want to see me squirming as I work out the implications of what would happen to my future if I attempt to save Yvonne's life; what would happen to me and Trisha. You'd like to see me destroying my mind if I had a real "butterfly flaps its wings, hurricane somewhere else" scenario, wouldn't you? Nice try, but none of this is real is it? I couldn't do anything about Yvonne if I wanted to, could I?"

"Not real? You look pretty real to me. That's a real cheese and tomato sandwich you're gesturing with."

"I mean it's just a very clever fabrication. Yes, I'm really here and I'm sure you've got Trisha here somewhere, but it's not my real past, just a brilliant fake. Very impressive, by the way."

"Thank you very much. What gave it away?"

"The pot of roses, or rather what Carla said about them. I didn't buy those from the market the first time round. And the newspaper article about young Patricia Hallam. They were just bait to lead me to you."

"Very good, but completely beside the point. You went through a lot of stress and torment while you figured all that out, didn't you? Which is what my client wanted. Therefore, my work here is done."

"What?"

"Well if you're going to go on beating yourself up and wallowing in guilt, there's no point me adding to it. Waste of my time, and quite frankly, a waste of yours too. That's up to you though. As I said, my work is done."

"So what happens now?"

"Well I suppose you'd quite like to go home."

Parallel Wives

Melanie Rainham, nee Robinson, was growing more frustrated with every passing hour. After years, so many years, of waiting for Chris to suffer retribution for his cold-hearted lack of concern for her cousin, finally something was happening. But now she was just waiting, practically tied to the telephone, to hear if her demands were actually being carried out. Why did a vengeance demon insist on using a landline? She was becoming very agitated and she needed a chamomile tea.

Trisha Adwell, nee Hallam, was growing more uncomfortable with every passing hour. After her doubts, so many doubts, she realised she's in Chris's dream, suffering from the cold and a lack of food. She had no idea why this was happening, but there was nothing practical she could do but wait, tied to a chair, and wondering if anyone could hear her demands to be freed. Why did her captor insist on using such a tight twine? She was becoming very agitated and she needed a wee.

On Yer Bike

I was only, at best, guardedly optimistic at the mention of going home. I knew there had been talk of a deal, but I wasn't entirely ready to trust everything my new best enemy said. It could merely be another opportunity to reduce the quality of my mental health.

"I would very much like to go home, and I'd like to take my wife with me if it's no trouble."

"Oh it's no trouble for me. I could just put you back where I found you."

"But you're not going to, are you?"

"Certainly not. Where's the entertainment in that? No, you have to find your own way back."

"Good grief. You don't make anything easy do you? I'm so glad somebody's enjoying this."

He got up: "Come on. I'll point you in the right direction. Give you a clue; something even you might recognise." He hurried towards the door, calling to the man behind the counter, "Put that lot on my tab, Charlie. I'll sort it out later."

I followed a few paces behind, wondering what he'd meant when he said I was going to have a big day. As if yesterday wasn't big enough. Needless to say, the town I see before me as I step outside the coffee shop isn't the one that was there when I went in. Here we go again. I'm guessing that this will be the "Leeds" of my dreams; it's the only place I ever dream about. The demon turned to face me.

"Okay Mr Adwell. This is where we part company. Live long and prosper."

"Isn't that Star Trek, not the Bible?"

"Yes, alright! I mix them up sometimes. That's the problem with science fiction."

Strangely, in spite of my frequent bursts of animosity towards him, I'm not looking forward to being on my own again. And he's certainly not what I imagined a demon to be. I suppose they must get sick of people always assuming horns and a tail.

Surprisingly, he's holding out his hand for me to shake and equally surprisingly I find myself reciprocating.

"It has been a pleasure to meet you, Mr Christopher Adwell. You've been very good company."

I'm not sure I'd go quite that far with the reciprocation, but he could've been worse. And that second espresso was superb.

"I'm not sure what I was expecting from meeting you, but it wasn't this; certainly not an interview with a demon. Who the hell are you? And where are you from?"

"Ah, these existential questions that you humans love to ponder. Would it make any difference if you had the answers? I very much doubt it. You don't even know where you're from yourselves. Thousands of years of arguments between the god fearing creationist lot and the evolved ape crowd and no agreement arrived at. So never mind all that, or who I am. You've got today to find your way back to your future, so you can go and live out your remaining miserable thirty years or so in something like the manner you would prefer."

He had a very carrot and stick approach to conversation I thought; helpful, encouraging, rude and dismissive. But time, I had to agree, was probably pressing, so I simply said, "So what do I do now?"

"Just follow your dreams, my friend, follow your dreams."

I couldn't quite see the relevance of him going all inspirational fridge magnet on me, and I said so. He points to a bicycle propped up against a wall, and then at some arrows, the sort of signage I was familiar with back in my sportive riding days. Ah, now I get it.

"I said I'd give you a clue, but I'm not here to make it easy, so after that you're on your own. I can't be expected to do everything for you, surely. I think you'll work it out as you go along, and I believe it is written that the worker is worthy of his wages. You seem like a bright lad, occasionally. Now if you'll excuse me I've got to go and settle up with Charlie and then report back to my client."

"You reckon you've done enough then?"

The demon is distracted, leafing through a Bible that he has produced from inside his capacious coat. "Luke, chapter ten," I hear him muttering.

"Sorry; had to check. No, I don't suppose she'll be happy, but I never really wanted to take this on in the first place. I don't usually deal with small fry like you. No offence. This was doing a favour for an old friend, who unfortunately died recently. I'm rambling! You'd better get started or you'll never get home."

I walked over to the bike, which wasn't exactly a dream machine. The demon spoke again;

"Now go and get lost. That's what usually happens in your dreams." Then he vanished back into the cafe and I never saw him again.

Living The Dream 3

It is said that you never forget how to ride a bike. This saying cannot be adapted to cover bike maintenance; whoever owned this specimen had forgotten to put enough air in the tyres or lubricated any of the moving parts and I didn't imagine they would mourn its passing too much if I borrowed it, as per the demon's instructions. In any case, if this experience I was about to have was based on any of my dreams I wouldn't be saddled with the dilapidated wreck for long.

I remember how this goes. I've been given the transport, now I need to follow the signs until the next link in the chain of events presents itself. I don't feel like I'm exactly geared up for whatever new obstacles may lay ahead, but I'm hoping that adrenaline and the prospect of seeing my wife again will see me through.

Obviously my first priority was to find Trisha. I had no idea what had happened to her or what state I would find her in, but my recent conversations had left me optimistic that she would be found. I needed to get my bearings and look for the clues that the demon spoke about, starting with the arrow that he'd pointed out to me. The bike rode as badly as it looked, but it was at least marginally quicker than walking. I set off in the direction that the first arrow indicated, which took me along a straight road away from the hub of the busy town and into a suburb with a mixture of commercial and rather run down residential properties, shabby blocks of flats.

The next arrow turned me left at a fork in the road and past more drab office buildings. God, some of my dreams are really boring, I thought. Then a more chilling thought grabbed me: not all of my dreams are boring. The one where I finished up in Auschwitz wasn't! Please don't tell me that's where he's put Trisha. Would he really be that cruel? I tried to balance the strangely civil hour or so that I'd just spent with him against the maniacal glee he'd displayed in my dream as he'd ushered me and my family to a hideous death. How well did I really know this guy? A code of conduct, a dislike of swearing and poor table manners and the assurance that none of this was personal, that he was just doing his job, didn't rule out the likelihood that he was a sadistic bastard with a very warped sense of humour.

The butterflies in my stomach started performing like a gymnastic display team when I saw a sign pointing to a railway station up ahead, but then stood down again and took a breather when I realised that the arrows I was following turned me away in another direction, for which I was initially grateful. But gratitude soon changed to puzzlement. For some reason the arrows diverted me from the main road into a cemetery. I really hope I'm not going to find my wife in a cemetery.

I've always found cemeteries intriguing places; so much history, and I have sometimes found myself frittering away time, sidetracked from my own life, reading the inscriptions on the stones, the birth and death dates, sometimes information about how or why they died. And it makes me sad to think of all these people who are now absent from our lives, but whose existence on the planet was every bit as relevant and important as mine. We're all dust in the end.

This is a huge graveyard here in the suburbs of "Leeds" or whatever fictional location the demon has placed me in. The bike rattles along, gathering speed as it rolls down a gradual slope towards an area with rows of stark white gravestones. They all look very new. In the middle of this section a woman is kneeling, placing flowers on one of the graves. A bunch of yellow roses. Well what else would they be? She straightens up, and a chill goes through me. It's Yvonne. I should be used to being shocked by now, but no.

I squeeze hard on what passes for a brake on the bike and slam my feet down on the ground with such force that I'm nearly thrown off. Yvonne, or whoever or whatever she was, surely another demonic fabrication, looked round at the commotion. I knew my mission wasn't going to be easy; I just didn't know it would be this hard. In the absence of any furniture, I fell to my knees.

"Chris! At last. You're looking well."

"I am?" I didn't feel well.

"Well, perhaps a little pale right now. Get up off your knees, Chris. It's much too late for begging." I struggled to my feet and she turned away. "Come and see this."

I followed her back to the grave she'd been tending. I'd already guessed it would be her own. The words on the stone read:

Yvonne Robinson
Much loved daughter and granddaughter
Taken too soon

"What do you think of that, Chris?"

"I don't know what to say," and then, in contradiction of that statement, "I loved you too," as if, for a moment, I were talking to the real Yvonne.

"Did you? Hmm. Clearly not enough. I loved you, but not any more."

"No. No, I can understand that. I didn't know….."

"Oh, it's not for anything you've done. No, it's because I'm dead. I don't love my parents or my grandparents any more either. I can't, because I'm dead, thanks to you." She gestures towards the inscription again. Her parents and grandparents; and how many other people had been affected by her preventable death? Could she make me feel any worse?

"What do I do now? What can I do?"

"Nothing. You can't save me, if that's what you mean. It was never an option, as I think you've already figured out. But I've waited a long time to show you this. And I never could get used to waiting for you, could I? No, you just go back to your easy, comfortable life, where you're everybody's friend, just like the old days."

"I'm sorry. I thought….."

"Don't! Just don't…...Better get back on your bike. Your wife will be waiting, just like the old days."

"Yvonne! Look…." But she was gone. One moment I'm trying to work out what to say to somebody who can't possibly be real, who may or may not be a figment of my imagination or who may be someone or something constructed to torment me, and the next moment there's nobody to talk to; she suddenly vanished, not even a footprint in the grass. I just stood there, shaking as if I'd seen a ghost. Had I? I don't know what I'd seen, but I knew there was nothing in what she said that I hadn't said to myself countless times already. That brief encounter didn't actually result in much of a conversation, but it was enough to make me feel crap about myself again.

I finally picked up the bicycle and scanned the path through the cemetery, searching for the familiar arrows. I'd almost been distracted from the mission to find Trisha. Having found the way out, I continued my journey through the dismal landscape, which, true to my dream that this episode seemed to be based on, took me straight through the open door of an office block. Feeling grateful for this merciful diversion, I recollect that in my cycling dreams I would ride up the first couple of flights of stairs, but this old boneshaker certainly didn't have the gearing for that kind of stunt. I'd be glad to see the back of it anyway. So I leaned the bike against the inside of a window, very carefully, as if either the bike or the grimy window in the deserted building were worth something. After my graveyard encounter I was feeling more fragile than the glass. I began the trek up the staircase on foot.

The building was, to all intents and purposes, disused, it seemed to me, and by the amount of dust and grime and typical ephemera of an abandoned office block, the plastic cups and sandwich wrappers, it had been empty for some time. I kept climbing, without any real idea of where I was going, just assuming that there would be some indicators eventually. At each new level I would stop and call out my wife's name, but there was only silence. I tried all the door handles. Many of the doors were locked and the ones that weren't only opened onto empty rooms. By the fifth floor

I was beginning to flag a bit. There's only so much energy you can get from two small coffees and a Chelsea bun, and I wished that I'd eaten all of the cheese and tomato sandwich. I decided to take a breather and stood for a couple of minutes looking out of a window, which wasn't made particularly easy because the window was as dirty as the rest of the building. I picked up some bits of discarded newspaper to clean enough of the window to allow me to see out.

And lo and behold, one sheet of the paper had the story that there were still no clues in the search for the missing Durham University student Patricia Hallam. Was he just trying to mock my inability to find her? That wouldn't surprise me either; at the moment I felt like my whole life was being ripped to shreds by criticism. I folded the sheet of paper and put it in the pocket of my jacket. If we ever get out of this it will make a very interesting souvenir. I noticed as I reached into the pocket that I still had my phone, which hadn't been a whole lot of use to me during my stay in 1991 and still wasn't. The battery didn't have much charge left, and it occurred to me, out of nowhere really, that I'd never seen a drama on TV where the participants had to stop to charge their phones.

I rubbed a circle in the grime on the glass, sufficient to give me a view. I found myself looking down on a row of terraced houses and at the next clue, so obvious that even the dimmest amateur sleuth, and I'm not sparing myself here, could recognise it. Moving in the breeze behind a half open window were faded orange and yellow curtains. What with all that had been going on in the last couple of days they'd slipped to the back of my mind, but they pretty sharply elbowed their way to the front again.

What I had to do now was find a way down again. I felt as if I had to keep the house with the curtains in sight. I had a notion that if I retraced my steps to the front door of the building that everything would have changed and I wouldn't be able to find the house again. That may not have been logical, but I know what my dreams are like and I wasn't at all sure that this distorted reality would be any different.

Approximately ten feet to the left of the window was an emergency exit door. There wasn't anybody to evacuate at this stage of the building's life, which was just as well as it was blocked with a battered old filing cabinet and a dried out yucca plant. The filing cabinet didn't have much in it, just a couple of yellowing bits of paper, probably risk assessments for evacuation procedures. So it was easy to move. The dehydrated plant offered little resistance and the fire door opened as fire doors should. I stepped onto the top step of the fire escape and then rapidly stepped back again. The metal of the top platform had patches with as much structural integrity as cornflakes or any of the other available breakfast cereals. As much as I wanted to make a quick descent to the house I had seen from the fifth floor, there was no advantage in racing down and breaking my neck. I reckon a fall from this height would probably kill me, although I don't like to jump to conclusions. I thought perhaps that coming up with a pun about falling to my doom would cheer me up, but not this time. I'll write it into my memoirs at some point; hopefully there will be some time in the future to look back and laugh about it all. Hopefully.

I made slow progress, testing each of the steps that weren't actually missing, for their load-bearing capacity, pausing to see if each metallic creak meant that the whole structure was about to part company with the wall and daring myself to contemplate what would happen if it did and, in between the moments of painfully hesitant action and the moments of panic, looking down to see if the curtains were still flapping in the breeze.

What should have been the last flight of this precarious steel staircase was missing, most likely removed by a trader in scrap metal or by somebody who considered that a large metal ladder was wasted being stuck on the outside of an empty building and they could find a better use for it. Crawling to the end of the last solid platform and lowering myself over the edge so that I could safely drop the last few feet to the ground wasn't doing much for the condition of the clothes I had acquired from Carla's wardrobe. I dropped into a scrappy looking bush that had enough springiness to soften my landing and enough thorns to lacerate the backs of my hands. As I stood on terra firma and attempted to brush off bits of rust and twigs, I realised that I must have left my Roger Waters' tee shirt back at Carla's.

That presents some interesting situations: would it be recognised as a valuable bit of merchandise that would fetch a fortune on a yet-to-be-invented online auction site? Or would Carla just tear it up for cleaning cloths, angry when she discovers that I haven't gone to the doctor's and I've deceived her again? Or was the whole scene I've just lived through merely a demon manufactured charade? Could well be, but I've definitely left the shirt somewhere. Do I have to work this out now? I'm under considerable pressure dealing with the present, or what passes for the present right now. Would that sentence even make any sense if I wrote it down?

Vengeance demons clearly move in mysterious ways. I was glad to have avoided any encounters with pitchforks, fire and brimstone, but I was starting to find the moving goalposts on the trail I'd been set, something of a torment. When I arrived at the house, I discovered that the window had been shut, the curtains no longer moving in the breeze. Was whoever had closed it still inside? The door of the house refused to budge when I tried it and pounding on it produced no response either. I backed away from the house, as if widening my angle of vision would make any difference to a locked window and door. Glad I did though, because that was when I noticed, about five doors down, a second house with those same bloody curtains. Sometimes I can be as sharp as a tack, so I didn't hesitate to head off in that direction, only to find, as I approached that house, that there was another one a little further on, identically curtained, and then another, and then…..

This went on for a bit, round a corner into an even further down-market street and the backs of houses rather than the fronts. Was this a demonic idea of a joke? Ah! No. The next bit was the joke. I came to a house with red curtains. Ha bloody ha! A stop sign?

The demon had said I would figure it out and I figured out that the red curtains implied that I should go back to the previous house. Do demons play Monopoly? He was definitely sending me to a property on the cheaper end of the board. Another thing; I'm right off curtains. I will be getting quotes for vertical blinds, roller blinds, anything but curtains, when I get home. Or if, of course…..

I backtracked to the previous curtained house and then I knew at once that this was where I would find Trisha. If I hadn't been in such a hurry following the trail I would have recognised the back of this house from my dreams. There was the crumbling garden wall that I climbed from to access the nondescript little room I had dreamt about being in so many times. Resigning myself to the conclusion that my clothes had lost any shred of what is called sartorial elegance that they may once have had, due to climbing down from one building, I put it way beyond doubt by scrabbling up another one. Really, the odd snagged button and ripped knee didn't matter much compared to the urgency I felt to get in and rescue my wife. She'll be in a right mood!

The old sash window slid up like a dream, and I squeezed through and landed as an ungainly heap on the threadbare red carpet. Levering myself upright, I'm facing a wooden dresser with the inevitable pot of yellow roses, a bit withered now; I know how they feel. The other figurines are there too, as anticipated, the children having a picnic and the cheesy blue tit. At the end of the room the door stands slightly open, the door leading to a room which had caused me such unease in my dreams. I'd never been in there and had always made sure I headed away from it as quickly as I could. But this time I was drawn to it by muffled sounds of stress and complaint.

"Trisha!"

The muffled sounds grew in volume and I pulled the door open and rushed into the room. Trisha was, of course, there, tied to the only piece of furniture in the room: a huge armchair. At least the demon had given her somewhere comfortable to sit, so it could have been worse. She had been gagged, though, with what was by now a very soggy piece of black cloth. I was so relieved to see her and I hoped the feeling was mutual. She immediately started to try to speak through the gag. Obviously I couldn't work out what she was saying, only catching the last syllable, which sounded like "ee". I bent down and reached round the back of her head to remove the gag. Velcro! How thoughtful. Then her words rushed out:

"I desperately need a wee! Does this place have a bathroom?"

"How should I know?"

"Well it's your fucking dream house, isn't it?"

I was able to concede that point and work on her other fastenings at the same time.

"Try that door there." I helped her to her feet and she hobbled off in search of a loo. I had no exact knowledge of how long she'd been tied to that chair, but she must have a bladder like a steel trap. Clearly there must have been some kind of functional plumbing in the house, because she returned looking a lot less agitated and we were able to carry on with our delayed happy reunion. The "I love you" and the "I've been so worried" were somewhat tempered by the unsurprising fact that she was more than a little angry and confused. Unlike me, she had no idea what this was all about and she hadn't had the benefit, if that's the right word. of my discussion with the character that had engineered all this. It was probably a bad time to say that I had to grudgingly admit his superb eye for detail in his recreation of my dreams.

"What the hell's going on Chris? What the devil is all this about? First you vanish without a trace, then I wake up on that bloody chair."

Devil wasn't a bad choice of word, I thought.

"Hard to explain really. Unbelievably hard. But the short story is that I've really pissed somebody off somewhere in my past and I'm being punished for it. It's something to do with either my first wife or the woman I left her for."

"What? The one that killed herself? That's crazy! So why do I wake up tied to a chair? What's it got to do with me?"

"I think it's more a case of that putting you in danger just added to my stress, rather than you being punished for something you've done. I think...Look, I don't even know who it is."

"You're joking!"

"I'm not joking. I have no idea who it is, except that the person is female, which narrows it down to about half the population. Could we speculate later, after we've got out of this dump, do you think?"

With that I led the way back to the room I'd climbed into and walked over to the window.

"Now last time I was here I climbed out of this window and managed to reach the top of that wall over there. It's a bit of a stretch.."

"I'm not climbing out of any bloody windows. Bugger that. We'll go the other way. There's a staircase just past the bathroom and it leads down to the front door. Much more sensible."

It was. Much more sensible. Once on the pavement outside I employed distraction techniques, like some animals do in moments of stress, brushing the last few bits of leaf and rust out of my hair and clothes, while I tried to work out a way of presenting the far from sensible sounding account of my recent activities, and that the way out of this mess was be directed by some supernatural being's advice to follow my dreams. I remembered my own horrified reaction to finding myself trapped and isolated in my past life. Was it only the day before?

"Chris, I was terrified when I found you weren't at home. I couldn't understand how you'd got out of the house. I still can't."

"I don't really know exactly how myself, and I don't want to scare you, but there's a very powerful force making all this happen; the same force that left you tied to a chair."

"You don't want to scare me, but you tell me this is, what? Something supernatural?"

Reluctantly, I told her that this was certainly the case. We're a couple of devout atheists who have never held any kind of belief in the spirit world, whether they're the good guys or the bad guys, so to speak. There might be some spadework needed before I tell her that I've spent an interesting morning having coffee with a vengeance demon. On the other hand…..

"Before I found you in that room, I spent an interesting morning having coffee with a vengeance demon." I could tell that she didn't immediately know how to respond to that; speechless, so I thought I'd add some more detail. "It was him that told me how to find you."

"That's ridiculous!" Why do my wives, ex or current, use that word when I tell them something they don't understand? "What's a vengeance demon?"

"He was the old man from my dreams. At least, that's what he looked like today."

"Still sounds ridiculous to me."

"Alright. Do you have a better explanation? Let me guess; you went to sleep at home and woke up on that chair in a house that previously featured in one of my dreams. If you can think of some way that would happen without some kind of force beyond our day to day experience then…."

"Where did you wake up? Tied to a chair?"

"I woke up in a chair, yes, but not tied to it."

"Oh well that's nice. Let me tell you that several hours tied to a chair is no fun."

"It could've been worse, I suppose. I mean at least it was a comfy chair, not a wooden one…"

It's as well the demon wasn't there at that moment to hear my wife express her opinions on my last comment. I was sure he would have had very strong views on women swearing, especially in the street. When her burst of anger subsided into a kind of a sobbing, which I thought was completely justified after the experience she'd been through, I delivered some more food for thought, even harder to digest.

"I woke up in my old house. In 1991. I met Carla and Stevie again. And we're still in 1991 I think. Look at the cars, and that phone box, with an actual phone in it."

Trisha looked dumbfounded. I'm sure if she hadn't recently developed such an aversion to furniture, she would have looked for something to sit on.

"Is there any chance that phone works?" she asked.

"Probably, but who do we call? I doubt if we'd get through on any 07 mobile numbers. If we call the police we'll probably finish up on a vagrancy charge looking like this. I mean, do you want to tell them this story?"

I elaborated on my recent journey into the past and how I had finally managed to meet the old man of my dreams. Or from my dreams; sounds better.

"It gets worse. About an hour ago I met Yvonne too."

"What?! Chris, what the hell's going on. You told me she killed herself."

"She did. I found her putting flowers on her own grave. It wasn't really her. Either that demon orchestrated it all or I'm having stress induced hallucinations. Either way, I feel like crap. Whoever's behind all this…. this persecution is getting their pound of flesh.

"You're telling me that somebody is out to get you because you didn't stop your mistress from killing herself twenty seven years ago? Is that it? Why wait so long?"

"I get the impression that was the first chance the demon had to fit me into his busy schedule."

"You're kidding me! How very business-like. I'd like to give this whatever-he-is a piece of my mind!"

"Yeah, I'm sorry you had to spend so long tied to that chair."

"Never mind the chair! It's this whole damn messing with our lives thing! Invading our dreams! How do we know it won't all start again when we go to sleep?"

174

"Er...because he told me he was finished with us."

"And you trust this malevolent arsehole?"

"I think we can. Well I thought so, but I wasn't expecting him to inflict the Yvonne experience on me, so I'm not a hundred percent confident. But he did tell me how to find you and said we'd get home. And he would report back to his client, job done."

"Job done? Somebody's put a contract out on us with a hit man from another world or something? Who would do that?"

"I have no idea, except that it's somebody, some woman, who has some kind of connection with Yvonne and presumably is still alive, because he said he was going to report back to her. He did say that she might not be very pleased."

"About what?"

"About him deciding that I'd suffered enough; a combination of all this shit that he's been inflicting on us and me beating myself up for years already."

"So he says he's stopped, but there's no saying what this bitch that he's working for might do? I can't deal with not knowing who this is. Didn't you tell me that Yvonne had a friend who was very angry with you?"

"It's not her. I asked him that; she seemed the most obvious, but he said no."

"And of course you believed him. Sounds to me that you actually like this demon. God! Listen to me! I'm talking like this is all normal."

"Well I have to say, I can think of people I've had business lunches with who were much less pleasant company. Do you think, one day, we'll look back at all this and laugh?"

She looks at me as if I'm an idiot. It's good to see her old self returning gradually, the sarcasm and everything:

"If I hear any laughing in the next couple of months there'll be trouble. So how did this character that you've chummed up with suggest we get home? Or is he going to send a taxi?"

"He said to follow my dreams. I know. Sounds corny, but it's brought me this far. We just need to look for the next clue."

"Oh. perhaps we should split up and do that then! More bloody curtains I suppose."

I looked up and down the street, but I couldn't see anything to suggest a way out of this dingy neighbourhood. A tandem leaning against a streetlamp would've been a dead giveaway, but there was nothing. And then we heard a dog barking from the end of the street.

"Well look who it is," said Trisha, almost, but not quite, laughing. "Time to follow my dreams this time I think."

If You Want Something Done Properly...

Just who did this Mr Bloody E, or whatever his sodding name might be, think he was, deciding that Chris had suffered enough? Surely that was her prerogative, not his. Who's the client here? Twenty seven bloody years he'd made her wait, twenty seven years of being patient, of playing Ms Nice Guy, of watching Chris flaming Adwell moving forward with his comfortable life with his oh-so-lovely wife. He might think he'd got away with murder, but, oh no! If you want a job doing properly, give it to a woman.

Melanie remembered that the demon had asked her, the very first time she'd met him in Joyce's library, why she didn't just pour paint stripper on his car or poison his cat. Well she had, years ago, when she felt like nothing was happening, but it wasn't enough, not by a long way. The demon had rebuked her for interfering in his "master plan". Master plan! Another decade had gone by and now Adwell was being let off the hook.

She was furious after the useless Mr E had called her at home to tell her his decision to cease punishment, angry enough to call him Mr E before she slammed the phone down. He'd informed her that the Adwells were on their way back home, from wherever it was he'd taken them; he didn't tell her that. A bloody holiday camp compared to what she had in store for them. Before she went to the Adwell's house to deal with car and cat, the new car and cat, she drove well out of town. It gave her time to think, time to plan her next move, and she didn't want to bump into anybody she knew while she was organising the welcome home surprise.

A village supermarket with a petrol station gave her exactly what she needed; petrol for the car plus some more in a plastic container, ("It's for my lawnmower. Oh, and some antifreeze too please."), and she was pleased to see that they sold lemonade in glass bottles. That took her back a bit. She could just about remember a van coming round the housing estate with those. Lemonade, dandelion and burdock, cream soda. And there was money back on the bottles. Whatever happened to that very environmentally sound idea? Never mind; these two bottles weren't going back.

I Don't Usually Like Dogs

The pink dog with the green lead stood at the end of the road barking at us, waiting for us. We didn't require a consultation to decide that we should follow the animal and as soon as we moved, so did the dog. The only drawback in our pursuit, and a major one, was that, before being lifted from her sleep and deposited in the armchair, Trisha had taken her shoes off. As it doesn't fall within the remit of vengeance demons to provide footwear for their victims, I assume, she still didn't have any shoes. Our progress was slow. She made reasonable progress on smooth tarmac, but then the dog took us over a long section of rough ground. I tried carrying her for a while and, though I put it on record that I am making absolutely no derogatory comments about my wife's weight, not wishing to incur a fate worse than anything a vengeance demon could think up, it wasn't easy. Carrying babies and toddlers up to the age of three is easy. After that, it's a struggle. I kept stopping to rest, with comments about not being as young as I used to be, to which came replies about trading me in for a younger model that didn't have such weird dreams. We tried the piggy-back, but Trisha decided it wasn't very elegant. But what a patient dog! It never really allowed us to draw close enough to catch hold of the lead, but it wouldn't run too far ahead either.

Our bizarre trio, an impossibly coloured dog, pursued by a man with torn and generally dishevelled clothes, every now and again carrying a woman with no shoes, attracted occasional attention from people we passed. Maybe this happens all the time round here, wherever here is. The route took us through a suburb and through a shopping area, all busy with people shopping or gardening or washing cars, typical early evening activities. A queue at a chip shop made me realise that we hadn't had any substantial amount of food for some time and Trisha and I were both flagging, running out of energy. She'd had even less to eat than I had.

"Don't suppose you came out with any money on you?"

She grimaces, "In my pyjamas?"

"Thought not. I've got £10 in my phone, but it's one of the new plastic ones and I have a feeling it won't be legal tender just yet."

I watch people throwing their fish and chip wrappers into a bin.

"How hungry are you?"

"I'm not eating out of that bin, if that's what you're thinking."

"No, I was wondering about the bins of the supermarket next door. Do they just chuck out perfectly good stuff that's gone past its expiry date? Did they have expiry dates in 1991? I'm going to nip round the back and find out."

I didn't wait for Trisha to object on the basis of health and hygiene, but nipped round the back as promised, safe in the knowledge that CCTV wouldn't have been a monitor of my actions, even if I was unsure about use by dates.

Not a great deal of thought had gone into recycling, major concerns about our environment being a much later development. Overlooking the general air of decay and neglect that the paying customers were never meant to see, I made my way to a huge blue skip which contained all the cast off packaging and general detritus from the supermarket. I hoped it included some packaged food. Sure enough, there were sandwiches in plastic wrappers, but I knew Trish wasn't all that keen on white bread, especially the blue-spotted variety. But I did find a couple of Cornish pasties in unbroken and airtight condition which were among that day's rejects. A reconstructed 1991 with sell by dates; amazing attention to detail. He's very good at his job, our demon. Our demon?

That measly haul would have to do. I didn't think Trisha would enjoy being left on her own in this strange place for any longer than absolutely essential. I wouldn't say she was very impressed with what I'd found. She inspected the integrity of the wrapper carefully, checked the sell-by date, asked me what today's date was, which, amazingly, I knew.

"April 18th."

"How the heck do you know that?"

But then she complained,

"It's not very vegan."

We were as close to being non-choosy beggars as we've ever been.

"Right now? Sod vegan. It's got potatoes, carrots and onions in it."

"Good point. I shall eat my semi-vegan food gratefully."

We found a bench to sit on to enjoy our al fresco dining. Well, the dog found the bench. It seemed to sympathise with our need for a rest. I wondered if it could get us into a b'n'b for the rest of the night, because it was starting to grow quite cold. I've always liked the idea of road trips, but the romance of this one was starting to elude me. I threw the last scrap of my pastie to our colourful canine guide.

"Not bad, that. Not bad at all. I shall have to raid bins more often." Then, thinking out loud:
"Must be ages since we had a night out together."

"Ha bloody ha. Look, I'm dying to get home, but I don't think I want to spend the night stumbling about in the dark, cutting my feet to ribbons."

Where do the homeless go at night? How do they cope? I didn't relish the idea of settling down in a shop doorway for the night, but then I didn't imagine that those who were doing it on a nightly basis thought it was great either. I hoped that I would never take my home and secure sleeping arrangements for granted again, but these sentiments wouldn't solve our immediate accommodation crisis. It wasn't quite dark yet; just about light enough to see that the pink dog was on the move again. We had little choice but to drag ourselves off the bench and resume walking.

He didn't take us far; about two hundred yards to a car park behind the supermarket. There were a large number of cars and vans, presumably a mixture of shoppers' and town residents' vehicles. The dog stopped in the far end of the car park, next to a scruffy looking Ford Granada estate car. This had clearly come a long way from its glory days in a showroom, but the cracked windscreen, expired tax disc and below pressure tyres indicated that it wasn't going any further any time soon. Its best feature was that the door locking buttons were in the up position. I took a furtive look over my shoulder and then opened a rear passenger door. Another thing that had long gone was the new car smell, replaced by something that was hard to define, but if we wanted shelter for the night we could probably get used to it.

Trisha didn't look very keen, but the combination of cold, dark and now suddenly, drizzle had her pushing past me and climbing onto the Granada's capacious back seat. Adding to my comment that it had been a long time since we'd had a night out together, I observed that it was even longer since the evening had finished on the back seat of a car.

"You can forget that idea, unless this car has an en suite bathroom!"

So I forgot that idea, and we snuggled up close together, hoping that our combined body heat would make the next few hours of darkness tolerable enough to get some sleep. We nodded off listening to the light rain pattering on the roof. The dog had made itself comfortable by crawling underneath the car.

We woke just as it was getting light. Even a big car can be an uncomfortable place in which to sleep, and we were cramped and stiff, in need of a good stretch and a couple of toothbrushes. We compared dream notes and were extremely pleased to find that neither of us had had any. Perhaps our demon really had given up.

"Chris, what was it like going back to your old life? I mean how did you feel meeting Carla and Steve?"

"God, that was strange. Kinda sad."

"Do you wish you'd never left?"

"No, not sad about that exactly. I mean I'm happier where I am now than I've ever been. Not in the back of this old wreck; I mean with you. I love you, you know that. I feel like my being with you was finally a mature, balanced, logical relationship, not like…."

"Excuse me! Try not to leave all of the magic and romance out of it. You sound like Mr Spock! Not logical, Captain."

"Sorry. Give us a kiss! That's the second time I've had Star Trek quoted at me today. No, it's just coming face to face with all the damage and realising how much hurt my actions have caused. Then I realised there was nothing I could do to change what's been done. And I don't like hurting people."

"I know you don't, love. Although, it's probably fair to say that all of this is happening because you had an affair, and before you butt in, I know all the whys and wherefores of it. We've talked about it over and over again. Not a problem. Consequences though, eh?"

"Are you trying to tell me something?"

"Just that I never realised it was possible to enlist the services of a vengeance demon, but I do now."

She gave me a reassuring squeeze and then pointed out of a window. "Looks like Pinky's moving us on again."

"Okay. Incidentally, before we go, you weren't ever abducted while you were at uni and forgot to mention it?"

"What?!"

I told her about the newspaper article, and then I remembered that page that I'd kept as a souvenir, the one I found in the office block. She was intrigued and horrified;

"He's even got my name right. I don't like to think about somebody or something knowing so much about us…..we should frame that though."

"Terrifying, isn't it? I wonder if this goes on all the time. Probably best if most of us stick our heads in the sand. Come on! The dog's on the move."

I looked at the supermarket's skip as we passed. It was too early for a fresh delivery of not very fresh food, so we elected to skip breakfast, and hoped that home wasn't too far away. The demon had told me I was going to have a big day, not spend the rest of the week walking, and we'd already delayed somewhat with our overnight sleep.

"Are you ready for another day as a refugee then? The past is a foreign country, they say, we've only got the clothes we stand up in, our money's no good here, and my phone's useless."

"That's not like a refugee. They all seem to have phones these days."

"Cynic"

.

We had no idea how far we had to go and the suburban roads went on for miles. Felt like miles, anyway. Suddenly, Trisha cried out:

"Look! That archway! That's the one I saw in my dream. I hope to God it leads us back into the town." That seemed to give her renewed vigour. She's definitely taking this dream business seriously at last. I followed on, optimistic as well, and also doing my bit of hoping to God; hoping that the demon had got the year right. If we arrived home in 1991 we wouldn't have a business to go back to for one thing.

It turns out that we didn't have a business to go back to anyway. As we followed our canine friend through the archway we were indeed back in our own town, back in the good old High Street, back in our own time. And not one hundred yards away was our hardware store, receiving the attention of a considerable number of firefighters as they toiled to bring an intense blaze under control. Over the crackle and roar of the flames we could hear occasional explosions as the heat reached our stock of camping gas bottles. And the sound of more fire engine sirens, but strangely, going away from the town not towards it.

There was clearly a limit to how closely we could approach. Perhaps it was just a good time to stand and get a bit emotional, so we did.

The number of onlookers grew and grew, developing on the principle that nothing attracts a crowd like a crowd. Most of them we knew; small town life is like that. Friends and acquaintances came over to offer their commiserations because of the fire. Nobody commented on our appearance. Perhaps they thought we'd been at the shop, fire fighting, before we handed over to the professionals. I didn't think that many, if any, would have known about our disappearance. We'd only been gone a couple of days. A much needed short break would account for that if necessary.

"Chris, look there isn't much we can do here, and I could really do with getting washed and dressed. Can we just pop home and sort that out first?"

That made a lot of sense. I looked down at her poor feet; she would definitely benefit from being treated to a pedicure. I might try for a double appointment; her feet, my back. We set off on the short walk-cum-hobble in the direction of home, only to be greeted by another acquaintance who looked very stressed and pale.

"Trevor! What's up?"

"You can't go home. I'm so sorry."

"What are you talking about?"

"Your house has had a fire. It's really bad."

We became a bit more emotional. Well, I did. Trisha had fainted.

No Place Like Home

I've never had any personal experience of a property fire before. That is, I mean having my house burn down was something of a novelty. I imagine that feelings about losing your belongings may well depend on where you were at the time. If you were actually in the building and struggled to escape death or had to be rescued from the smoke and flames, you might consider your material possessions to be of little importance compared to your life.

But not being in a life threatening situation gave me a different perspective and I mourned the loss of all the familiar objects that made our lives comfortable, bits and pieces with sentimental value, things we'd had since childhood and gifts we'd bought each other; all gone. Well, mostly gone. The fire at our home had centred on the downstairs rooms, so that was my hi-fi, my record collection and the sofa reduced to nothing before the fire brigade could do their stuff. Somebody sure knew how to hurt me! The top half of the house was extensively smoke damaged. I know I'd been thinking about a wardrobe makeover, but perhaps not quite so soon.

The police informed us that the fire investigators had yet to officially declare the exact cause of the two blazes, but arson was strongly suspected.

No! Really?

We knew that our insurance company would step up to deal with the practical and financial side of our crisis, as undramatically as possible, but they wouldn't be able to replace our cat. Trisha asked the fire crew if they'd seen any sign of the animal, dead or alive. Animals have a sensible attitude towards fire; they run away if they can and we assumed that had happened because there was no trace of her in the building.

I'd gone from one day of overwhelming mental overload straight into another. Our business premises were ruined, our staff had no jobs, our house was uninhabitable, our clothes were inadequate, our car keys were melted, our cat was missing, a demon that I'd trusted had gone back on his word or his client had taken matters into her own hands, and we were both very hungry and in need of a shower.

Small town hospitality being what it is, we had a fair few offers of temporary accommodation to help us for as long as we needed it. We were offered everything from spare rooms to granny flats to house-sitting while the owners went on holiday, food, drink, clothes, transport. People's generosity was some consolation, which was much needed.

Trisha, after her initial fainting spell, had required quite a bit of consoling, an expression that fits the criteria of Classic British Understatement. But it didn't take long before her mood moved onto anger: furious, livid, mightily pissed off.

For the want of any better target, she directed this at me.

"This is all to do with your bloody dreams, isn't it?" which must have been a very difficult question for anybody overhearing it to understand. We were in a friend's spare room, about to avail ourselves of their en-suite facilities, and it's possible they did overhear, given the volume of Trisha's outburst. I could tell she was in no mood to be shushed either, but fortunately she must have realised that if she continued in the same vein to express herself on the subject of vengeance demons or spiteful harpies we would be getting moved on to more secure accommodation with those padded cells we'd been joking about not that many days earlier.

Although her recent experiences had moved her out of the sceptical category when it came to other worldly dream manipulation, now that we were back in the normal world, or at least a world that's as normal as it can be when you've suddenly lost everything that you own, she was struggling to believe what she was saying.

"I'm struggling to believe I'm saying this. Because of some incident that happened nearly thirty years ago, we've been targeted by some creepy being from another world, he's put us through all kinds of shit and then he burns down everything we own. It's ridiculous!"

"But he said he'd leave us alone…...I can't believe I'm saying that either."

"People are going to be wondering, aren't they? It doesn't take a genius to rule out coincidence. What am I going to tell my mother?"

"Speaking of which, my phone's charged up again. Did you want to ring her before the jungle drums beat you to it?"

"God, no! Not yet. I need a shower first."

So while she did that I called Steve, who was all full of concern and offered us a stay at his place, which I said we might take him up on after we'd dealt with all the local stuff and needed to get away. It would do us good to see some family again. It was weird talking to him about going to stay with him. Last time I saw him, about a day or so ago, he was heading off to preschool. There would be a police investigation to cooperate with first and insurance claims to submit. A whole load of etceteras really.

I was surprised that Melanie hadn't been in touch, but then thinking about it, she didn't usually ring me, but rather Trish, and Trisha's phone was undoubtedly as functional as our car keys and record player. I thought I'd take the initiative and phone her instead, but the call was cut off as soon as it was answered. These things happen. I tried again, with the same result. Odd, but I wasn't going to spend all day doing that. I was sure we'd catch up later.

Trisha came out of the bathroom, towelling her hair and looking very fetching in somebody else's dressing gown. Looking very preoccupied too.

"You look like you're thinking about something."

"I've been thinking." (I was right) "If this so-called demon of yours was acting on behalf of somebody else, then who was it? Do you know anything you're not telling me?"

I decided not to make a thing out of whose demon it was, which I assume is not the same as demon possession, but just told her the scant details that I knew.

"He said it's a woman who had some connection with Yvonne, a close enough connection to make her extremely hateful I suppose. That's it."

"So she's got to be at least in her forties and knows where you live."

"Knows where I used to live!"

"Don't remind me. Come on! There's not much of the day left. I want to go back and see if I can find the cat," which, incidentally, never had a name; just, The Cat. It was getting on a bit now, the kitten that Trisha had chosen from Melanie's litter on the day they first met.

We grabbed a light early evening snack from one of the local pubs, which the sympathetic landlady insisted on paying for, and then we set off in the direction of Ye Olde Cindered Cottage, attempting to get there before we ran out of light and energy. As much as it was good to have the sympathy of friends and other assorted well-wishers, we were thinking that some sort of disguise would be useful so we could get somewhere without stopping every two minutes to have a "how are you coping? and if there's anything we can do" based conversation. Being ungrateful and impatient is the only way to get anything done today!

Everybody needs one nosy neighbour. For the people that live in our street it's usually me. I'm definitely a curtain twitcher, noticing every out of place car and white van that cruises by. My own personal nosy neighbour is the bloke who lives next door. What a pair we must make, comparing registration numbers and descriptions of swarthy looking drivers who obviously didn't grow up round here. No, it's not quite that bad, but as we walked down the road that afternoon, he came out of his front door, having already twitched his curtain. I can't believe

I'm even thinking about curtains after all that I've been through with them.

"Chris, Trisha; how are you coping?"

"!"

"I've got some more bad news I'm afraid. We've found your cat, but she's um.....I'm sorry"

I put my arm around Trisha's shoulders. She's not taking the news at all well, understandably. She loved that cat.

"Thing is, it doesn't look like it had anything to do with the fire. She was in somebody's greenhouse, all stretched out."

Our mission was accomplished, but not in the way we wanted, obviously. We retrieved our pet's body from the back of man-next-door's house, which he'd thoughtfully placed in a cardboard box lined with an old blanket.

"Don't worry about returning the blanket. This is a bad business, right enough. Can't think who'd want to do a thing like that, setting them fires and doing that to your cat."

"Don't suppose you've seen anybody about the place? Anybody suspicious?"

"Can't say I have. There's just been that lady that came in yesterday morning. Said she was here to feed your cat while you were away for the two days. I reckon she's gonna be right upset too."

"The lady....? When was she here? And definitely the one you've seen here before?"

"Yeah; tall blond lass. She let herself in yesterday morning, like I said."

I don't know, under the influence of the planet's gravity, at what speed a penny drops, but on Planet Adwell the coin was very reluctant to fall. We Adwellians were standing looking at each other, not at all keen to be the first one to say what we were thinking. Trisha broke the silence.

"Why did Melanie think the cat needed feeding? I never said anything about going away. The day before I woke up on that bloody chair she said she'd be round to see me in the morning. And then she's telling the neighbour we've gone away. I don't understand."

"And what I'm thinking is, a woman in her forties who knows where we live. But I don't understand either. She's practically your best friend; she can't possibly be the person who's done this to us. Can she?"

"It doesn't make sense, Chris. I've known her almost as long as I've known you. She moved here not long after we did.....You don't think she followed us, do you?"

"Only insofar as we both lived in the North before we came here. The north of England is a big place. It isn't a village. I did try phoning her earlier while you were in the shower and the call seemed to be answered and then cut off. Didn't think anything of it at the time, but now, I don't know."

"What do we do? We've hardly got anything to go on and it's all a bit unbelievable. We can't text her and ask her, and I don't want to report her to the police, not without being absolutely sure. She could be completely innocent."

"Okay, so if she genuinely thought we'd gone away, for argument's sake, and she knows nothing about the cat or the fires, why hasn't she been back to feed her today? To me, it looks dodgy. Somehow she knew you weren't going to be there, and you didn't tell her that."

As if life hadn't handed us a big enough bunch of uncertainties, we now had a suspect, an unlikely suspect, but precious little evidence to allow us to point the finger with any conviction. Besides, we had urgent matters to attend to, like asking the local vet to establish what had killed the cat, and our first proper interview with the police, who needed to investigate the arson attacks. That could all wait until the next day. First of all, we needed a good night's sleep, preferably without too much in the way of dreaming. Not that I ever got a choice.

So we said goodbye to our neighbour, sad to be turning our backs on the ruins of our home, sad to be carrying the remains of our cat, and sad to be so unsure about the trustworthiness of somebody we thought of as a good friend.

The Force Is With Us

Being exhausted is no guarantee of a good night's sleep, especially when you have the number of dilemmas to face that we had, never mind a proven reason for being nervous about dreaming. I don't like sleeping in strange bedrooms either. Strangers' bedrooms? No; still coming out wrong. I mean rooms that aren't mine. The bed's all wrong, or the heating and ventilation aren't right, or the light. Grateful, but picky.

We did manage to sleep a bit and in the morning, neither of us could remember dreaming; again. Bonus! Our hosts were a couple in their sixties and sensitive enough not to badger us with questions, and they did make remarkably good coffee too. Not all of my problems could be solved with coffee, admittedly, but at least their coffee wasn't added to the list of problems.

Our first appointment that morning was at the vet's to drop off the cat for examination, and then back to our temporary accommodation, where we had arranged to have a first chat with the police, a detective-sergeant and a constable in uniform. The uniformed officer spoke first.

"Hello again, Mrs Adwell. We met the other day, you remember."

"Ah yes! When my husband, um, couldn't be found. Thanks for all your advice."

"No problem. Glad everything turned out okay. Are you feeling better now Mr Adwell? Your wife called us to say you were unwell."

"I did what!?"

"You called the non-emergency number the next day to say that Mr Adwell had turned up at the A and E, but then you were going away for a couple of days. I'm sorry you've had to come back to such a mess.......What? Is something not right?"

"I made no such call."

"Look, I know you've had an unbelievable amount of stress over the last couple of days. Is it possible you've forgotten the call?"

"Excuse me, Constable, but my wife definitely couldn't have made that call. We were...away. I don't suppose you have a record of where the call came from."

"Not on me, but I can make a call and get somebody to check the phone records."

The plain clothes officer looks a bit puzzled and speaks up;

"Are you saying, Mr Adwell, that you didn't have a bit of a medical episode?"

Thinking on my feet, or rather on my hosts' dining room chair, I replied,

"Yes, a touch of brain fade, I think, and I've had a doctor's appointment to put everybody's minds at rest." I didn't mention that the doctor's appointment was twenty seven years ago and that I hadn't turned up for it, but never mind. I very much wanted to get them back to the theme of investigating two clearly related conflagrations.

Trisha and I were exchanging glances whilst trying to look as if we weren't. We didn't want the police to suspect that the fires were our very own insurance scam. If I were a copper, I'd probably have arrested the pair of us by the end of the day, because our story was full of holes that were going to require some extensive creative thinking to fill in.

For a start, I'd kind of lost track of how many days we were gone. It had seemed like only two, but throw in an almost triple decade scene shift and, well I just don't know.

If we had gone away for a couple of days, as our flimsy cover story suggested, how come our car was still in the garage, probably extensively fire-damaged by now, and the keys a molten blob in the porch? How did we get to where we were going, and how come, when we came back from this mystery destination, was Trisha in her bare feet and night attire? Must've been quite a party!

Maybe I could get my son to say he'd driven down and taken us to his place to rest up, but I didn't really want to start lying, or involve him in lying either, even though that might be easier for the police to swallow than the idea that we'd been abducted, while we were asleep, by a vengeance demon and that we're starting to think one of our best friends is behind it all.

Motive! That would get us off the hook. Everybody knows we love our house, and we're very happy with the shop. All we need is a few upstanding character witnesses and, ta-dah!...case dismissed. Anyone who knows me well would know I'd never set fire to my record collection. That would be the clincher. I can imagine the judge and even the counsel for the prosecution in tears when I tell them about the vinyl perishing in the flames.

While I was busy defending and cross-examining myself, I became aware that the police constable had returned from his call for information and was speaking to me.

"I have obtained the information that the call to our 101 line came from a landline yesterday morning. The number was your home phone and the caller identified herself as Mrs Adwell. Do you still say that you didn't make that call, Mrs Adwell?"

This was clearly a bit of a pivotal moment. If she said that it had probably slipped her mind and that she must've made the call then it wouldn't tally with our story about being somewhere else. If we stuck to the couple of days away version they would want to know who could've made the call. I'd go for option two, but I wasn't the one being asked the question.

At that point my phone rang and I made a big show of answering it to give Trisha a bit more thinking time. Personally, I was ready to throw Melanie under the bus, but Trish might be able to think of a different answer.

The call was from the vet, confirming our fear that The Cat had been poisoned. A blood test had indicated ingestion of ethylene glycol: antifreeze. It could have happened accidentally; cats are attracted to the sweet smell and taste, but two fires and a poisoned cat? Come on.

I passed this news on to the room. Trisha was very upset and the police were very sympathetic. I'm sure policemen, in their private lives, are just as soppy about pets as the rest of us. But their professional side realised that the vet's news put another piece in the jigsaw puzzle of their investigation.

"Can you tell us, Mr Adwell, if anybody else had access to your house yesterday? A woman, perhaps? Somebody who could have phoned us from your landline."

Trisha and I looked at each other and I shrugged. Trisha replied,

"My friend Melanie. A neighbour tells me she came in yesterday morning to feed...to feed the cat. Melanie Rainham. We've been trying to contact her, but she hasn't got back to us yet."

"Is that unusual? Not replying, I mean."

"Yes, I think it is."

"Okay. Well I think we can let you know that the fire investigation officers found signs of suspicious activity at both of your properties. There was broken glass on the inside of the shop window, some of it from what it is believed is a bottle and they sent in one of their dogs, which reacted to the presence of an accelerant. It seems that somebody threw a bottle of petrol through the window late last night."

"A Molotov cocktail!"

"You could say that. Petrol was detected in your house too, but whoever did it had attempted to be a bit more sophisticated and had laid some kind of a crude fuse that eventually set fire to the curtains. We think that happened before the shop fire."

I didn't mourn the passing of the curtains.

"Not all that sophisticated if you're a known key holder and the neighbour sees you at the house."

"Indeed not, Mr Adwell. Also, your car is still in your garage, but it's been covered in paint stripper. Right, so we shall ask your neighbours if anybody saw this lady later in the day. Meanwhile, I think we need to have Melanie Rainham's contact details, if you don't mind."

As they headed for the front door to leave, the detective turned, Columbo style,

"Just one thing we didn't cover; if you weren't at home when the call was made, can you account for your whereabouts?"

I decided to opt for the lie which I'd rejected earlier. It sounded feasible.

"Yes, my son Steve picked us up from the doctor's appointment and we stayed with him at his place near Birmingham for a day or so. It was good to see the grandkids again. Then he dropped us in town because he was late for a meeting in Swindon."

Good one, I thought. A bit of embroidery I'd been working on. There followed a brief staring competition, which I won, and the policemen left to continue their investigations elsewhere. I closed the door and went to the bathroom to bathe my tired eyes, and as we were just about to do a debrief on our conversation with the police my mobile phone rang again.

It was Melanie's husband, Greg.

"Chris! I've just heard the news about the fire at the hardware store in town. It was on the radio. And your house too? Are you both okay?"

"We're okay. A bit shaken up, but we weren't there so…."

"Sorry to butt in mate, but have you seen Mel at all? Just that she went out last night and I haven't seen her since. Getting more than a bit worried, to say the least."

"Last I heard for definite, Greg, is that she went to our house yesterday morning to feed our cat." I thought I would proceed very cautiously with this conversation.

"Oh Jesus! A police car's pulling up outside. I hope nothing's happened to her. I'd better go."

"Okay, well call us if you need anything. We're here for you, mate."

I brought Trisha up to speed with the latest development. I had a feeling that Greg was in for something of a shock. There was nothing of the criminal mastermind about him, although, to be fair, I could hardly believe that Melanie could have anything to do with this either. But then, if not her, who? I was trying to think of anything in our friendship with this couple that might be a clue, some sort of indication that she would want to do us harm. She had always been a good, reliable friend. Trisha wasn't a great one for girlie nights out, but when she did occasionally indulge, it would be with Mel.

Mel was the one who enthusiastically delivered my dream interpretations. That's not much to link her to my dreams, but, hang on; what was it Greg said about her? You never knew if you were going to get beads and flowers, something like that, or crucifixes and pentagrams.

"Trisha! That night we were round at Mel's and she did all the dream stuff; Greg came in from the rugby club, pissed as a rat. You remember he was telling us about when they first got together? Tarot cards and stuff. What was it he called her, can you remember?"

"Oh I don't know. Wasn't it The Divine Miss R, or Ms R? Definitely a letter."

"God! I didn't think anything about that at the time, because their name's Rainham. But that was before they were married. She wouldn't have been Rainham then. Idiot!"

I called Greg back, not too concerned about how his interview was going.

"Chris, what the fuck! What's the big idea sending the cops round here? My Mel's not an arsonist!"

I didn't want him to get too worked up; "I think they're just trying to talk to anybody who was at the house or might have seen something. Don't worry."

"I am fucking worried. I have no idea where she is."

"I'm sure she'll turn up. Listen, Greg. What was her surname before you got married?"

"What the hell kind of question is that right now? I need to get back to the police, mate."

"Greg, you called her the Divine Ms R. What did the R stand for?"

"Jesus, Chris! I've gotta go. Let's do the pub quiz some other time, eh!"

"Greg!"

"Robinson! Alright? Happy now?" And he put the phone down.

No. Not happy at all.

Take A Seat

I relayed this information to Trisha and, I have to say, at this point, I was feeling pretty low. What the exact connection to Yvonne was, I still had no idea, but just the thought that somebody we had accepted into our lives as a trusted friend had been effectively stalking me with who knew what end game in mind, was really distressing. The demon had said she didn't want to kill me, just make me suffer. That's some consolation.

"Where is she now, Chris? That's what worries me."

"Exactly what I'm thinking. And is destroying all our property enough, or are there more shocks to come?"

"We need to tell the police about this; the Robinson bit, I mean."

I can hear a phone ringing somewhere in the house, followed by footsteps on the stairs and a discreet tap on our bedroom door.

"Chris, there's a gentleman on the phone downstairs, and he's asking to speak to you."

"Oh thanks, Jenny." I follow her down the stairs and pick up the phone. "Hello?"

"At last! The Lord may not tire out, nor grow weary, but seriously, how long does it take to get to the phone? Mr Adwell, I think you owe me a cup of coffee. Unless your local café does special rates for pensioners; in which case I'll buy my own. I notice that your landline isn't working, for obvious reasons, so I've had to use this one."

Everything we've got on our plate at the moment, and now a Bible obsessed bloody vengeance demon to deal with; one that won't use a mobile phone for some reason.

"I thought you were going to leave me alone."

"And so I have. Now shut up and listen. Not everything's about you. It's taken me ages to find a phone box that wasn't either full of books or defibrillators."

"Have you never thought of getting a mobile?"

"Certainly not. They lead to obsessive behaviour and there are still concerns about microwaves and brain tumours. Only a fool would take that risk. Someone like you. Now, again, shut up and listen. Do you want me to deliver you from evil or not? This is about my former client, Mrs Rainham. I surmise her identity is no longer a secret, am I right? I don't take kindly to being contradicted and when I informed her that she no longer required my services, she, how would you put it? She lost it. Went off on one, to employ the modern vernacular. I have to say, like the dragon in the book of Revelation, I am growing rather wrathful with this woman"

"Why? Not why are you growing wrathful; I'm fairly pissed off myself. I mean, why did any of this happen?"

"I think you've discovered that there's a connection between her and your erstwhile lover. yes? Mrs Rainham was Yvonne Robinson's niece and held her in very high esteem. She has always blamed you for her death. A bit like you do, except she wasn't prepared to brush it under the carpet like you did. I fear she has become more than a little preoccupied with making you pay."

206

I thought 'more than a little' expressed it very well.

"So why are you here? We've told the police that we think she's involved and they're taking care of it."

"Very commendable I'm sure, but the police won't find any evidence that she started the fires. All they can prove is that she went to feed your late lamented cat. She can claim a legitimate reason for covering the house in fingerprints. She's clever. Not as clever as me, obviously. But nobody saw her go back later."

"How do you know that nobody saw her?"

"What a stupid question! Why do you, of all people, ask how I know this or that?"

"Fair point."

"Of course it's a fair point! But of greater concern right now is that I know where she is now and the police don't."

"Where is she?"

"Sitting in her car, just across the road from young Steve's house."

"What!" I nearly dropped the phone. Trisha, whose curiosity had led her to come downstairs and join me and was listening too, clutched my arm in shock.

"We need to call the police now."

"Well I foresee a couple of problems with that idea. They might ask who your remarkably well informed source is. Call that problem A, if you will. Problem B is that there isn't time. She's there now. So, would you like to engage my services to act on your behalf? Clean this mess up for good."

"What's he saying, Chris?"

"Well, basically, would we like a vengeance demon to go and sort Melanie out for us before she goes and does something terrible to Steve and his family?"

It could be said that hell hath no fury like a woman who has just discovered that her best friend has been pulling the wool over her eyes for ten years. It's not the pet poisoning or the arson or the possibly murderous intent she minds so much as the deceit.

"Let me talk to him."

"My wife wants to talk to you."

"I know." I hand over the phone.

"I don't know who or what you are, but I'm very angry with you. Don't interrupt!" Wow!

"Being stuck in that chair was horrible. What did I do to deserve that?"

"Oh, well I apologise that you didn't enjoy the chance to have a sit down. I constantly hear people, especially women, moaning about being rushed off their feet."

"Not funny….but you sure know how to hurt a girl. So if you want my vote, go for it. Find that bitch some furniture!"

Trish hands the phone back to me. She looks flushed and warlike.

"Your wife has introduced democracy into our conversation. What do you say?"

"What's going on up there?"

"I can just see Steve's lovely wife; Chloë, isn't it? She's walking the kids home from school. Mrs Rainham can see them too. And she still has a can of petrol in the back of her car."

"Right! Do your worst. Or your best." Depends on your point of view I suppose.

"Unanimous then. I'd better get a move on. So, er, Chris; still okay with me calling you that? A pleasure talking to you both. Look after yourselves. He who loves his wife loves himself, according to St Paul, and I'm sure the reverse works too, although the bloke wasn't married, so I suppose he thought his ideals looked good in a scroll. Pompous ass. Anyway, I'm off to do something you're clearly completely incapable of."

"What's that?"

"Protect your family."

See? Carrot and stick, every time.

Epilogue

We gradually rebuilt our lives, our house, our shop; a couple of kittens. My self respect took longer. Still working on that. I expect I always will be. Nobody ever saw Melanie again. Another open police file, another family shattered. But sometimes I'm aware of her in my dreams, and sometimes the dreams are like nightmares where she's screaming abuse at me. But to all intents and purposes, she's gone. Or more accurately, as the expression goes, she's not gone; she's in the next room.

I could do with a sit down now.
There's a bit of Chris in me.

Printed in Great Britain
by Amazon

84059514R00129